Lin Carter is one of the most popular and prolific American authors of science fiction and heroic fantasy. In the latter genre he was one of the creators of 'Conan the Barbarian', central figure in a series of novels and story collections which has sold over four million copies throughout the world. His own fantasy hero, 'Thongor of Lemuria', has survived a series of six books and features in a popular American comic book.

Mr. Carter's interests in fantasy extends into more scholarly areas as well. He is the editor of a series of fantasy classics, including the work of authors such as William Morris, Lord Dunsany, G. K. Chesterton, and William Hope Hodgson. His book, 'Tolkien: A Look Behind *The Lord of the Rings*', was the first full-length study of the famous creator of the hobbits, and his book 'Lovecraft: A Look Behind the *Cthulhu Mythos*', provided an extensive study of the great modern American master of the macabre. More recently, 'Imaginary Worlds', published in 1973, has proved to be the only comprehensive history of fantasy in modern literature.

Mr. Carter and his wife live in a huge old house on Long Island filled, as he describes it, 'with books and dogs and archaeological antiquities, and all the other things which interest us most'. Still in his early forties, Lin Carter is the author or co-author of sixty-three books.

Also by Lin Carter

JANDAR OF CALLISTO
BLACK LEGION OF CALLISTO

Lin Carter

Sky Pirates of Callisto

Futura Publications Limited
An Orbit Book

An Orbit Book

First published in Great Britain in 1975
by Futura Publications Limited
Copyright © Lin Carter 1973

Dedicated to William Dutcher and
the readers of 'The Jasoomian'

ISBN 0 8600 78302
Printed in Great Britain by
C. Nicholls & Company Ltd.
The Philips Park Press
Manchester

Futura Publications Limited,
49 Poland Street,
LONDON W1A 2LG

CONTENTS

Book Five: AGAINST ALL ODDS

INTRODUCTORY NOTE

It was a perfect morning for work. Outside, it was a raw, wet, blustery April day. But in my small study on the third floor it was warm and cozy. A cup of fresh coffee sat steaming beside the notebooks on my desk; I had just lit a cigarette; I reached over to scratch the soft furry folds behind the ears of my bull mastiff, Mc-Gurk, who had just settled down with a deep sigh of contentment in his accustomed place behind my chair; I was well past the halfway mark in the first rough draft of a new novel called *Conan the Buccaneer* and the yarn was beginning to flow along at a nice pace of its own. And the doorbell rang.

Downstairs I heard the other dogs wildly barking and the sounds of my wife going to the door. In a moment the door slammed shut and my wife called upstairs to tell me a package had come.

"At this time of day?" I wondered.

"Not the regular mailman," she called back. "American Express."

"Where's it from—what's the postmark?"

A long, suspenseful pause. Then—

"Pnompenh, Cambodia."

And I got no writing done that morning at all. . . .

It's funny how chance or sheer accident or blind

luck—call it by whatever name you will—plays so powerful a role in human affairs.

It was by a sheer quirk of fate that I had received, five months before, a strange bundle of manuscript from the other side of the world.

That first manuscript had been sent to me by an Air Force major named Gary Hoyt, then finishing up a tour of duty in South Vietnam. While in Saigon, Hoyt had shared a billet with a young American soldier of fortune, globe-trotter, and vagabond flyer named Jonathan Andrew Dark. The two had become fast friends. Dark was captaining a helicopter squadron flying mercy missions for the International Red Cross. Early in March, 1969, Dark vanished from human contact when his copter was forced down across the Cambodian border while flying food, medics, and supplies out of a temporary field near Hon Quan, which is about sixty-five miles north of Saigon and only some ten miles or so from the Vietnamese border.

Jon Dark's squadron had been en route to a small village farther north which had been hard hit by Viet Cong terrorists. Seemingly, his own copter developed engine troubles, which caused him to fall behind the rest of his squadron, and thus he was alone when he made a crash landing in the jungles of Cambodia.

The area in which he disappeared is one of the densest and least explored of all the jungle territories on earth. Routine search flights failed to discover the gallant young flyer. They did not even find the wreckage of his helicopter.

It *should* have been the end of the story . . . but it was only the beginning of a story far stranger and more astonishing. For out of those jungles in early August of that year, Cambodian natives emerged with a tattered bundle of manuscript marked with the name and address of Major Gary Hoyt, USAF. A covering note requested the finder to deliver same to Hoyt, promising that the finder would be paid.

The manuscript was handwritten in some sort of homemade ink, inscribed with a quill pen on crude brownish paper resembling old papyrus. It purported to be a first-person narrative by Jonathan Andrew Dark, and it told an incredible story—a story which, if true, was the most astonishing personal story in all the glorious annals of adventure.

Dark told how his copter was forced down by engine malfunction and crashed in a jungle river. Traveling overland, hoping to reach a friendly native village, he discovered a ruined stone city of the ancient Khymer peoples. Therein he found a strange well lined with milky translucent stone like Soochow jade, amid a ring of monstrous stone gods. That night a lambent beam of mysterious light beat up against the tropic stars from the jade well. Accidentally exposing himself to the action of this ray of sparkling force, Dark was strangely and wondrously transported by some unknown agent to the surface of an alien world which its inhabitants called Thanator and which he at length identified as Callisto, the fifth moon of the planet Jupiter. The remainder of the manuscript told of his remarkable adventures and travels on the moon Callisto, ending inconclusively.

Hoyt forwarded this narrative to me on a sheer whim. Dark, it seemed, had no family, no heirs to dispute ownership of this literary property, and Hoyt did not know what to do with it himself. He cautiously assumed it was a fantastic romance, a work of fiction his friend had been writing and had for some reason carried with him when he left on his ill-fated mission of mercy. Hoyt and Dark were both fond of fantastic adventure fiction of the sort Edgar Rice Burroughs wrote in the 1920's and that I have been writing more recently. Hoyt reasonably assumed I might be willing to pass judgment on this "novel" and, in fact, suggested I have it published if I found it worthy. I read the story, thought it a marvelously entertaining work of fiction, and passed it along to my editor at Dell, Gail Morrison, who promptly purchased the rights to it. Gail insisted on using my name as author, obviously placing small credence in my protestations that I had merely edited the book.

Naturally, I was intrigued by this mystery. I scouted around and dug up what small evidence I could. A helicopter pilot named Jonathan Andrew Dark had indeed vanished on a routine mercy flight in March, 1969, the International Red Cross informed me. That was the first bit of evidence. Almost as exciting was a stray scrap of Southeast Asian legend, found in a delightful book called *Unsolved Mysteries of Asia* (Macmillan, 1964). The author of this book, the English archaeologist Sir Malcolm Jerrolds, discussed the ancient Khymer empire of Cambodia, the enigmatic stone ruins of Angkhor Vat in the north, and speculated on native legends about another ruined city in the south, named Arangkhôr. This sounded amazingly like Dark's description of the ruined city he had stumbled upon, the city of the jade well.

Still and all, this was slender evidence at best, and circumstantial. I still regarded the manuscript as primarily a work of exciting fiction. But more corroborative evidence soon came to my attention. In January, 1970, I spent an evening with Major Hoyt. His tour in Vietnam concluded, he was on his way home for a leave, and had stopped off in New York to visit me. He brought me astounding news.

Did I know anything about a British archaeologist named Jerrolds? he asked. He had run into the man in Saigon, had told him something of Dark's story, and this Jerrolds had been most excited by the details Dark gave on the location of Arangkhôr. Jerrolds was on his way into Cambodia to do some excavating of supposed Khymer ruins in the southern jungles. . . .

To make a long story short, if you happened to see the December, 1969, issue of a periodical called *Discovery: the Magazine of Archaeology*, and you read an article entitled "Mystery City of the Khymer Kings" by the journalist Ramsay Edmunds, you already know that Sir Malcolm discovered the Lost City of Arangkhôr—right where Jon Dark said it was!

What you don't know is that Jerrolds made a second discovery, to my taste even more interesting than the first.

A second manuscript had appeared at the bottom of the jade well.

And Gary Hoyt had it with him.

The first manuscript told of Jon Dark's travels and adventures across the face of the Jungle Moon, Thanator, of his encounter with several of the Thanatorian races, such as the cruel race of corsairs called the Sky Pirates of Zanadar, and the Ku Thad, the Golden People, whose gorgeously beautiful warrior princess, Darloona, rules over the stone city of Shondakor. Because the Thanatorians could not quite pronounce Jon Dark's name properly, and called him Jandar, I put my own title on the typescript I edited from that first handwritten manuscript, calling the first book *Jandar of Callisto*.

In the same fashion, when I came to edit the second manuscript, I titled the book *Black Legion of Callisto*, after the bandit army that had seized control of Darloona's city. Jandar's struggle to free the city of his beloved princess from the savage warrior horde who had conquered it by stealth and treachery formed the central plot of the second manuscript. As the story terminated in a splendid battle scene, the aerial armadas of the Sky Pirates intervened and carried off the woman Jandar loved—the princess of Shondakor, Darloona herself. And thus, on this inconclusive note, the second book ended.

Dell Books liked it as much as they had liked the first.

But my wife and I were afire with curiosity by this time. If Jon Dark really crashed in the Cambodian jungles, as both Major Hoyt and the officials of the Red Cross assured me was the case—and if he really discovered a lost, forgotten ruined city in the unexplored jungles, which the eminent archaeologist Sir Malcolm Jerrolds announced to the world was really there—how much else of this astounding story might be true?

Noël and I determined to visit Cambodia and investigate the spot. Several letters and cables were exchanged between Sir Malcolm and myself; airline tickets to Pnompenh were reserved; we obtained passports and were getting our inoculations—when chance came into the picture once again.

Only a few weeks before the package arrived by American Express from Cambodia, the world had been electrified by the astounding news that Prince Sihanouk had been deposed while on a visit to France and that the Cambodian government was in turmoil. Communist incursions across the border from North Vietnam were increasing—there was a danger of internal war. And the State Department canceled our visas, warning my wife and I that until the Cambodian situation had calmed, they could not permit American civilians into so troubled and potentially explosive a country.

Day by day we had been following the news announcements. Communist incursions were swelling to the proportions of a full-scale invasion. Would President Nixon send in American troops to aid the shaky new Lon Nol government? Would Sir Malcolm and his team be evacuated from what might shortly become a war zone?

If so, my one tenuous link with Jonathan Andrew Dark would be severed. . . .

The package with the Pnompenh postmark was heavy and squarish. I opened it carefully, cutting through the cords and ripping the paper open.

It was, as I had half-expected but had not quite fully dared to hope, a large manuscript inscribed by a quill pen of some sort in watery homemade ink on crude brownish paper similar to old papyrus.

With it was the following note:

My dear Carter—

Enclosed is an unexpected arrival, Saturday last. Obviously some rhythm or schedule to the phenomenon—must begin noting down date and time of the appearance of the light ray in order to anticipate same. Sending this—hurriedly—downriver to the capitol in care of my trusty boy, Phuong—no time to read it myself.

Things in a positive uproar here, as you doubtless know. Rumors of armed Communist parties are rife, and may just be some truth to them—spent yesterday afternoon jabbering on the wireless to some government idiot who wants to evacuate all foreigners from the "danger zone"—as he calls it. All foolishness, of course—told the fellow I wouldn't hear of it. Just begun mapping and photographing the South Plaza area, taking rubbings of interesting carvings, etc.—lose months of work if stopped now. Not in the least afraid of a few Cong terrorists—natives frightened silly of these Khymer ruins anyway. Worked nine hours a day in the broiling sun at the Timnash dig in '58 with the Israelis and the Arabs popping away at each other and never got a scratch. No worse than that time in the thirties, digging up Solomon's temple in Abyssinia, when Mussolini's bully boys moved in with mortars and machine guns and such—simply told the blithering idiots to go play soldier somewhere else and let a man get his work done!

Many thanks for the issue of *Discovery*, which arrived at last. That fool Edmunds got his dates mixed up, but at least the pictures came out nicely. I shall do a book on Arangkhôr that will make them all sit up and take notice, I promise you! Turning up some astonishing stuff here, almost every day. Did you know that milky stone the well is lined with—stuff that looks like jadeite—is a *synthetic?* Seems to be organic, but need the facilities of a first-rate analytic lab to test the stuff properly. Synthetic organic crystal—amazing chemical achievement for such an early people. Your Khymer is an astonishing fellow—some of the engineering feats here are worthy of the Romans. Remind me to tell you of the underground aqueduct my second team has been digging up over in the Great Temple precinct.

Can't abandon all this work now—bloody fools, with their wars! This is the discovery of the century—horrible to think that one bomb could wreck it all.

Mailboat leaving—must pack this off to you now—more later if we all get out of this alive— are you still coming over? Leave your lady at home if you do—snakes, dysentery, and now Communists. Don't know which is worse!

In haste—

Jerrolds.

My transcription of the manuscript follows and is self-explanatory. Whether or not we shall have further word from the lone American on far Callisto is something only the future can reveal. I have had no further word from Sir Malcolm since the above scrawled note, and whether he is alive or dead—or forcibly evacuated from his beloved ruins—is unknown to me. Only time will tell if this story, too, will have a sequel.

If not, and if this is the last we shall ever hear from across the titanic gulf of space, it will be left to some unknown astronaut of tomorrow to discover the true ending to this astounding epic. Perhaps when, on some future day, we land a manned spacecraft on the surface of the Jungle Moon, separated from us by three hundred and eighty-seven million, nine hundred and thirty thousand miles, he shall return with the answer to the many questions which this book leaves unsolved.

Then, perhaps, we shall learn the end of the story.

Will it be a happy ending?

We shall have to wait and see, you and I.

LIN CARTER

Hollis, Long Island, New York
June 17, 1970

Book I

VOYAGE INTO PERIL

Chapter 1

ONE CHANCE IN A THOUSAND

When all is lost, the most foolhardy course of action becomes feasible.

When you have nothing more to lose—except, possibly, your life—even one chance in a thousand seems well worth the risk.

It was thus that we resolved upon the most absurdly dangerous solution to our intolerable dilemma.

It had been a year, perhaps a trifle more or a trifle less, since I had stumbled upon the Lost City of Arangkhôr, abandoned untold ages before in the trackless jungles of Cambodia. In that colossal stone ruin I had passed the portals of the Gate Between The Worlds. An unknown force, whose secret was still an unsolved mystery to me, had miraculously transported me more than three hundred million miles from the planet of my birth to the surface of a strange and beautiful and terrifying world of marvels and monsters—a world where black and crimson jungles sprawl under weird skies of golden vapor, lit by five glorious moons.

It was a world of barbaric splendor, that world of Thanator, where savage beasts and curious peoples vied for supremacy. Three widely different races of intelligent beings shared this Jungle Moon between them —three races locked in unending warfare.

Into the very midst of this planet-wide struggle, a mysterious force had thrust me, lone, friendless, ignorant even of the tongue spoken by the strange Thanatorian civilizations.

The first of the Thanatorian races I encountered in my travels was not even remotely human—a savage, merciless, warrior horde of monstrous and emotionless arthopodes called the Yathoon. Not unlike tall, jointed insectoid beings were they, their gaunt yet graceful limbs clad in shiny grey chitin, their expressionless faces glistening masks of horn crowned by weird antennae and eyed with huge jewel-like orbs, black and glittering.

By these inhuman creatures I was enslaved and under their emotionless tutelage I mastered the single language spoken by all intelligent beings across the face of Thanator.

While a slave of the Yathoon Horde, I made my first friend on the jungle world—Koja, the tall, stalking, coldly logical chieftain of the Yathoon, who did not even comprehend the meaning of friendship until I taught him the sentiment. And, as well, while a Yathoon slave, I met and came to love the most beautiful woman in two worlds—Darloona, warrior princess of the Ku Thad.

Escaping by Koja's aid from our slavery, we were again made prisoners, this time by yet another mysterious people, the Sky Pirates of Zanadar. Humanoid in very truth were the Sky Pirates, sharing the worst traits of mankind; these cruel aerial corsairs lived like vampires, preying upon the lesser peoples of Thanator, who lacked their scientific mastery of the skies.

During the months of my captivity, first by the Yathoon and then by the Zanadarians, I learned something of the recent events which had transformed the jungle world to a gigantic theatre of war. Darloona's folk, the Ku Thad, or Golden People—so-called from their tawny amber skin which was not unlike that of the Polynesian peoples of my own world—had been driven from their home in the walled stone city of Shondakor and all their domain had been conquered by a migrant bandit army called the Black Legion.

Whereas Koja and I became mere slave laborers, toiling under the whips of the Sky Pirates, the Princess Darloona was held as a valued guest of Prince Thuton, the brilliant and unscrupulous leader of the Zana-darians. Ambitious to extend his empire, Thuton dreamed of wedding the princess and of pressing his claim to her throne by waging war against the Black Legion, now ruling the kingdom of Shondakor. Half-persuaded that to accept Thuton's suit would win freedom for her exiled people, Darloona would not listen to my protestations of Thuton's innate villainy. At length I managed to escape the slave pens of Zan-adar, finding refuge in the house of a Ganatolian master-swordsman named Lukor. This gallant and chivalrous old gentleman, revolted by Thuton's villainy as was I, became my co-conspirator in an attempt to free Princess Darloona as well as the Yat-hoon chieftain, Koja. During this period of enforced inactivity, I learned from Lukor the secrets of swordsmanship.

After some time we did indeed rescue the woman I had come to love, and my friend Koja, as well; and traveled the breadth of Thanator in a stolen aerial vehicle, eventually rejoining Darloona's exiled people who were hiding in the jungles of the Grand Kumala. Alas, my princess was captured by the Black Legion ere we had combined forces with the Ku Thad warriors—whereupon I conceived of a bold and daring plan, entering Shondakor in disguise and joining the ranks of the Chac Yuul (as the Legion was called),

pretending to be a wandering mercenary swordsman.
A carefully timed plot to free Darloona from the
clutches of the conquering Legion and overthrow the
Chac Yuul by smuggling Ku Thad warriors into the
city via a secret route was interrupted and almost
ruined by a sudden attack upon Shondakor by Prince
Thuton's flying navy.

By an odd quirk of fate, however, we both succeeded
and failed. That is, we did indeed break the Chac
Yuul hold on the city of Shondakor, slay their leader,
and drive them from the kingdom—but my beloved
princess was seized in the confusion and carried off
by the vengeful and cunning Prince Thuton. For many
weeks now she had been held captive for a second
time in remote and inaccessible Zanadar, rightfully
called the City in the Clouds. And this time her captivity was not shared by friends able to strive for her
freedom.

For weeks now, ever since the battle that freed
Shondakor, we, the victors, had been sunken in a profound depression. While the dominion was ruled wise-
ly and well by Darloona's noble and courageous uncle,
Lord Yarrak, the citizenry of Shondakor mourned the
loss of their princess and cried out that she somehow
be delivered from the cruel captivity of the Sky Pirates.

Their determination to free Darloona was no less
than my own. Freedom in Shondakor meant nothing
to me, nor did life itself, unless I could share that freedom with the most beautiful princess in two worlds.
For the last words I had heard from Darloona's lovely lips, even as the flying vessel bore her into the skies
beyond my reach, was an avowal of her love for me.

It was a fortuitous accident that gave us a method
with which to attempt the rescue of Darloona.

During the three-way battle between the Ku Thad, the Black Legion, and the Sky Pirates, one of the remarkable aerial contrivances of the Zanadarian fleet had become partially disabled and was taken captive. The remainder of the flying armada had either returned safely, it must be assumed, to the City in the Clouds, or had been destroyed in the battle. Only one vessel had been left behind unharmed.

The daring scheme which I had at length decided to endeavor to use was, simply, this:

Repairing the aerial galleon, stocking it with loyal Ku Thad warriors, I would fly the aerial craft across the face of Thanator to the very gates of Zanadar, and, attempting to impersonate Zanadarians, we would assault the royal citadel and carry off our princess to freedom!

As I have already stated, there was one chance in a thousand that this audacious plan would succeed.

Whatever the risks, I was determined to make the attempt.

This desperate scheme I broached to my comrades only a few days after our victory in the battle against the Black Legion.

The loss of our princess in the very hour of triumph had plunged the victorious Ku Thad into a profound depression, mingled with a grim determination to somehow effect her rescue.

We were met in an upper council chamber, high in the lofty towers of the royal palace of Shondakor. About us, clearly visible through the immense crystal windows, the spacious city lay spread out.

Broad, well-paved avenues radiated from the palace, which stood encircled by parks and gardens at the very heart of the walled stone metropolis. The broad, tree-lined boulevards extended in every direction from the palace like spokes from the hub of a wheel.

Above, the strange skies of Callisto were a glowing canopy of golden mists, illuminated by no visible source of light. The distance of Callisto from the sun is so great that the sun is but a very brilliant star from the viewpoint of the dwellers upon the Jungle Moon. The mystery of the light source is but one of the numerous enigmas of this weird world to which I have never found the key.

The council chamber was cut from massy stone, faced with softly golden marble sculpted into a fantastic frieze of godlike forms. The floor was carpeted with glowing tapestries of ancient work and the oval table was one glistening slab of dark green malachite. At the head of the table sat the kingly form of an older man whose noble frame, molded in the image of heroic strength, was draped in superb robes which glittered with gems and crystals unknown to me. This was the Lord Yarrak, Darloona's loyal uncle and regent of the domain in her absence.

About the curve of the table sat five personages. First was the ancient Ku Thad sage and philosopher, Zastro, his lined face and snowy cataract of beard giving mute testimony to the many years of his service to the throne of Shondakor.

Next to him sat the Yathoon chieftain, Koja. The gaunt, skeletal limbs of the giant arthopode were folded uncomfortably in a chair designed for a human occupant, but the glistening horny ovoid of his expressionless visage, with its black, gemmy, compound eyes, revealed no sign of discomfort.

A noble young warrior was seated next to the chitin-mailed insect-man. His frank and open face, keen, alert eyes, and breadth of brow showed him for one of high birth and gentle rearing. This was the

Prince Valkar, a lord of the Ku Thad betrothed from childhood to Darloona. I had made his acquaintance while serving incognito in the Black Legion, as, indeed, was he. Both of us had enlisted in the bandit army under false identities, and both with the same purpose in mind—to bring about the freedom of Princess Darloona.

A lean, elderly man was seated beyond him, a man whose clear, tanned features and alert dark eyes denoted him as a member of another race than the amber-skinned, crimson-maned, emerald-eyed Ku Thad. Although his seniority was evident, this man held himself erectly, and his slender, well-knit limbs, disposed gracefully, revealed extraordinary strength and suppleness for one of his years. This was Lukor the Swordmaster, a Ganatolian, whose friendship I had won in the streets of Zanadar and from whom I had learned the most hidden secrets of the art of fence.

The last person at this council was myself. A grateful populace had awarded me with the high title of *komor* of the Ku Thad in recognition of my daring attempt to rescue Darloona from the clutches of Arkola, warlord of the Legion.

To this small circle I revealed my wild scheme whereby the freedom of Darloona might be achieved, with luck. In all candor, and although they desired to rescue their princess with a fervor no less intense than that which flamed within my own bosom, my comrades at first thought me mad with grief over Darloona's loss. For surely, said they in commiseration, only one driven beyond the extremities of reason would have seriously suggested so ludicrous and dangerous a plan.

I was forced to admit that my scheme did savor of extreme desperation, if not madness, at first thought. But I begged them to consider further, for it was my firm opinion that upon closer consideration it would reveal some glimmer of a chance for success.

The basic problem was a simple one. The City in the Clouds, you see, was most aptly named.

The Zanadarians had constructed their fortresslike capital upon the peak of a great mountain north of the Grand Kumala jungles. This soaring summit of solid granite had sheer cliff walls so smooth and unbroken as to preclude even the possibility of our leading a land-based army of invasion against it.

In fact, it was my considered opinion that it was a feat beyond human powers to climb that mountain. Neither one man nor a thousand could achieve the summit alive. The precipitous walls climbed sheerly from the dizzying abyss for thousands of feet without a break, a ledge, even a handhold. The greatest alpinist on earth would have quailed before attempting to scale that soaring pillar of rock.

It was this inaccessibility that rendered the city of Zanadar invulnerable to attack. From their mountaintop eyrie, the Sky Pirates could descend to strike at merchant caravans and defenseless towns at will, and their foes could not carry the battle back to Zanadar, for only the Sky Pirates held the secrets of construction of their remarkable flying ornithopter galleons, and only from clefts in the peak of the mountain on which their capital was constructed did the natural levitating gas escape—the gas which, pent under pressure between the double hulls of their sky ships, made it possible for their fleets to navigate the clouds.

These facts were widely known and were accepted instantly by my associates in this mad venture.

I then pointed out my contention that, trusting to the remote height of Zanadar to render their dominion impregnable, the Sky Pirates doubtless neglected strict guard and surveillance in other regions. And were an enemy force, disguised as Zanadarian corsairs, riding a Zanadarian vessel, to attempt to land in the Cloud City, it should logically find little opposition or even suspicion.

My associates were forced to agree to the logic of this supposition. It seemed indeed highly likely, although very dangerous.

"But Jandar," my friend Valkar objected, "what do you know about flying one of these sky ships?"

"Rather a bit," I replied calmly. "Koja and I served as wheel slaves on the Zanadarian flagship *Kajazell* during a flight from the great plains to Zanadar itself —we flew across the entire length of the Grand Kumala jungles. I thoroughly understand the mechanism of the wings, and as for navigation, doubtless that will prove a minor problem. The captain's cabin will, I assume, have charts aplenty."

"This is true," Koja assured our comrades solemnly. "But even I am forced to admit, Jandar, that there are more problems ahead of your venture than merely maintaining the vessel in flight and navigating it."

"What further problems, then, do you foresee?"

"Landing the vessel," he said. "While I think I remember the method well enough, from observations performed during our slavery at the wheels, we shall doubtless do a sloppy job of it, lacking the extensive training and superior experience of the Sky Pirates themselves. Will not it seem suspicious if we land our vessel in a blundering and amateurish manner—as we can hardly help but do?"

"Doubtless it would," I answered, "but my plan contains further details I have not yet imparted to you. It is my intention to deliberately fake superficial damage to the craft and, when landing, to pretend the ship is more greatly damaged than is strictly true. Thus we shall disarm any suspicions our clumsy landing maneuvers might arouse."

Koja pondered thoughtfully, his great black jeweled eyes inscrutable. "There is merit in the plan," he said at last. "It should be easy to break away fragments of figurehead, ornamental scrollwork, deck rails and rigging and thus create the appearance of considerable damage. It just might work. . . ."

Old Lukor the Swordmaster spoke up next.

"Lad, my heart goes out to you, and I will join the venture nonetheless . . . but have you thought all of this out carefully? When the flying galleons circle for a landing, they signal with colored flags, if it is day, and with colored lamps, if by night, giving their registry number, captain's name, and squadron designation. Surely you cannot know the code upon which these signals are based? And surely to attempt a landing without it will arouse suspicion?"

"Quite likely," I agreed. "However, I hazard a guess that the captain's cabin will also divulge a signalbook. And if not, we shall make certain that our artificial injuries are such as to make signaling impossible—break away all the rigging, for example, so that flags cannot be flown—cut away those portions of wingfront and bow from where signal lamps are shown. Something like this can be done, surely."

A final argument was offered by Lord Yarrak himself.

"What of the personal appearance of the crew and yourself?" he asked. "You will not in the slightest resemble Zanadarians."

This was true. The Golden People of Shondakor, with their lambent emerald eyes, blazing red-gold manes and amber skins are startlingly different from the Zanadarians, who have papery-white skin, lank black hair, and lusterless black eyes.

The difference between the races is so extreme that it is one of the many mysteries of Thanator.* However, I had, of course, anticipated this objection and was ready for it.

"A simple matter of cosmetics will take care of that problem," I said. "Surely a whitening cream can be used to give our complexions the Zanadarian pallor, and black paste will darken our hair. The corpses of the Sky Pirates slain in the battle will supply us with authentic uniforms."

No further objections were raised, and so it was agreed.

There was just one chance in a thousand that we should succeed in this fantastic imposture and manage to carry away the princess from amidst the very stronghold of her enemies. But even one chance in a

---

* Captain Dark refers to the peculiar fact that it should have been impossible for a world like Callisto, so very much smaller than the Earth, to have fostered widely divergent genetic groups to the point of creating very different races. Callisto is far smaller than our own Earth, whose diameter at the equator is 7,927 miles, as compared to the Callistan, which is a mere 2,770 miles. Earth has, therefore, a correspondingly greater land surface, split, moreover, into continents widely separated by great seas. On Earth, portions of humanity in early times could remain separated from each other for ages, permitting inbreeding to accentuate genetic variations to the point of creating different races which breed true. How this could possibly have happened on Callisto, with its far smaller land area, is an enigma. Callisto, according to Captain Dark's description, does not even have oceans, hence no continental divisions, and the different races live cheek-by-jowl. Theoretically, such racial divisions should be impossible on a moon as small as Callisto: but then, for that matter, life on so remote a world, which is five times as far from the sun as is our own planet and receives a minute fraction of the sunlight and heat which support terrene life, should be absolutely impossible. Whether the answer to any of these mysteries will yet be discovered by Jandar in his travels is as yet unknown.—L.C.

thousand was better than none. And even a chance so risky as the one I contemplated was worth taking, when the life of the Princess Darloona was the prize at stake.

"I am well aware that we will be voyaging into danger," I said. "However, we have won success before in the face of the most desperate odds, through bold enterprise. I cannot think that our luck will desert us now. But I will understand if any of you wish to withdraw from this mission. At any rate, Lord Yarrak must remain in Shondakor to administer his regency over the city. But if any of the rest of you would prefer to stay and help him in his task, just speak up. . . ."

Koja, Valkar, and even old Lukor the Swordmaster refused to be left behind on this mad venture.

And so it was agreed.

Chapter 2

THE QUEST BEGINS

Our work on the flying galleon began the following day. In this task, my most valuable assistance came from the old philosopher Zastro. I have called him by that term for lack of a better, but he was no ivory-tower intellect who spent his years puzzling out intricate moral dilemmas or mental mazes. Quite the contrary, Zastro of Shondakor was more akin to those philosophic engineers of terrene antiquity whose talents ran to problems of practical mechanics, like Archimedes, who devoted his genius to the contrivance of elaborate and surprising war machines dedicated to the defense of Syracuse, or the mighty brain of Leonardo da Vinci, that superman of the Renaissance, who designed everything from cathedrals and aqueducts to tanks and protohelicopters.

The help of a master intellect of Zastro's talent was imperative if we were to repair and fly anew the damaged ornithopter.

The cunning and resourceful warlord of the Chac Yuul, Arkola, had long anticipated such an eventuality as the aerial invasion Thuton of Zanadar had hurled against the walled stone city. He had devised a system of rooftop catapults as partial protection against the sky vessels. A well-placed stone missile from one of these rooftop war engines had smashed the control cupola of the galley in question. Grappling irons, securely hooked in the ornamental carvings, figureheads, and deck balustrade, had immobilized the powerless aerial contrivance, drawn it against the roof of a neighboring edifice, whence warriors of the Black Legion, stationed thereupon against just such an eventuality, had swept the decks of the captive vessel with a torrent of deadly arrows, until the last Zanadarian of the sky ship's crew had fallen to the barbed rain.

All had been slain aboard the ill-fated flying machine save only for her captain, a cool-headed, suave-tongued gentleman privateer of Zanadar, who had received an arrow through the shoulder. This officer—his name was Ulthar—was the only captive that had been taken alive during the battle. And he had a place in my plans, I must add.

It was not impossible that we might yet win his active cooperation in repairing, manning, and navigating the aerial galleon. Although thus far, it must be admitted, Captain Ulthar had smoothly but steadfastly declined to assist the foes of his nation, for which I could hardly blame him. I yet had hope of converting him to our cause, if only to escape the rigors of slavery that awaited all war captives. I had also resolved to take him with us on the expedition, although I intended to keep close watch on him, and have him under guard at all times.

At any rate, we toured the damaged and captive ship with an eye toward our chances of rendering her sky-worthy once again. At my side, old Zastro searched the vessel with quick, intelligent eyes that missed not the smallest detail. We strode the decks of the sky ship together, assessing the extent of the damage Arkola's catapult had caused.

"Ingenious! Fantastically ingenious," the old philosopher murmured as he leaned over the deck rail to scrutinize the complicated system of cables and joints and pulleys by which the jointed stationary wings of the flying ship worked.

I agreed with him profoundly. Although I loathed the Sky Pirates for their callous cruelty, their merciless rapacity, and their insatiable greed, there was no question that they were a race of engineering geniuses without parallel in the chronicles of two worlds.

The ungainly flying contraptions of the Zanadarians were like great wooden galleons, rendered fantastical with carved poop, fluttering banners, ornamental balustrades, and cupolas and gazebos. They hung aloft on slowly beating wings, buoyed up against the gravitational pull of Callisto by the powerful lifting force of the natural gas wherewith, under compression, their hollow double hulls were suffused. To the eye of the uninitiate, that so huge a ship could float weightless, plying the winds of this world as the ancient galleons of imperial Spain once plied the waves of terrene seas, seemed incredible—miraculous. But the secret lay in the ingenious construction of the vessel. It was not fashioned out of wood at all, but of *paper*. Every last inch of the flying galleons were made of miraculously tough and resilient laminated paper—hulls, decks, masts, compartments.

This secret rendered the construction of the sky navy of Zanadar no less miraculous, but at least understandable. The true miracle lay, I think, in the incredibly clever system of weights and counterweights, wheels and pulleys, joints and hinges, by which the ungainly and enormous jointed wings could be manipulated in a close approximation of the actions of a bird's wings and by which maneuvering and flight were affected.

Koja and I had labored at the slave gangs that powered the vessels of Zanadar, and we were intimately acquainted with the motive system used. But knowledge did nothing to abate my admiration for the genius that had created the flying contrivances. No scientific achievement ever perfected on my own far distant world equaled the fantastic achievement of the Zanadarian ships, although the immortal da Vinci had sketched out plans for just such wing-powered ornithopters in his coded notebooks. Even his genius, however, had failed to go beyond the conception to the practicality. The Zanadarians had turned the dream into physical reality, and despite all their cruel ways, I could not help applauding their amazing skills with an undimmed enthusiasm.

But now we would turn the productions of their own imaginative genius against them. For if only a flying galleon of Zanadarian design could penetrate the remote and cloud-wrapped fortress of the Sky Pirates, we had here the means by which it might well be possible to achieve such a goal.

"Ingenious it is—but can it be repaired?" I asked

urgently. The aged philosopher pursed his lips judiciously, then nodded firmly.

"I am confident of it," he assured me. "Look here, *komor:* the catapult missile sheared the control cupola cleanly away from the deck surface—but it did not breach the hull. The supply of buoyant vapor remains thus intact; it only requires that we reconstruct the pilot cupola anew and reconnect the cables."

"Can this be done?"

"Without question it can," he responded with a vigorous nod. "I shall assemble my students and disciples into a work crew, and we shall if necessary press into service every carpenter and wheelwright and mechanic in all of Shondakor. You will have your flying galleon in ten days, that I promise you!"

To a man whose beloved is the helpless captive of implacable foes and who is helpless to fight to free her, ten days can be an eternity. Such was the case with me.

I passed the time, however, in training a force of Shondakorian warriors in the techniques of flight. There were half a hundred and more of these gallant swordsmen, volunteers all, who were more than willing to risk their lives in the rescue of their beloved princess. Indeed, virtually every fighting man of the Ku Thad had volunteered to serve in the crew of the sky ship—even the aged warriors and those who had been sorely wounded in the battle that freed the Golden City from the grasp of the Black Legion. Lukor and Valkar and I had examined these aspirants, choosing the youngest, the most daring, the most skillful fighters, thus narrowing the selection down to a hand-picked regiment of seasoned veterans, disciplined and fearless and utterly dedicated to the rescue of Darloona.

These men, some of them, would serve at the wheels. The interior hull was hollowed, and there the hands of many men were needed to lend their strength to the wheel system that manipulated the jointed wings. Koja trained these men in the technique, while Valkar and Lukor and I trained the others in the manifold ship duties they must master if we were to navigate the skies of Thanator and arrive safely in the city of the Sky Pirates.

By keeping busy at such important tasks as these, I managed to pass the ten-day eternity more painlessly than I might otherwise. It still seemed like an eternity to me; but it did pass.

And at last we were ready to depart.

I had effected one slight improvement in the designs of the unknown Zanadarian genius, for I planned for an eventuality even he had never contemplated.

I had caused to be erected on the foredeck a catapult of my own design to be used in defending our craft against the actions of another galleon.

The need for such a precaution had never occurred to the Sky Pirates of Zanadar, for they were alone and unequaled in their mastery of the skies of Callisto. No enemy nation possessed the knowledge or the ability to design similar craft, and thus weapons for a ship-to-ship aerial battle were unheard of and unknown.

When I displayed my sketches for such a device to Zastro his keen eyes sparkled with appreciation, for he instantly comprehended the uses to which the weapon would be put. At the time he remarked that not only would the Zanadarians have no defense against the actions of my catapult, but they would be helpless to fight back.

Since we would be pitting the resources of our one lone flying ship against the entire aerial navy of the

City in the Clouds, the slight technological advantage
given us by the possession of this unique weapon
might well prove invaluable. And thus his craftsman
built the engine from my plans and installed it upon
the foredeck at the prow.

My knowledge of so antiquated a weapon may seem
surprising—for no terrene army has employed such a
device since the Middle Ages. But in my boyhood I
was fascinated by the ingenious military weapons perfected by the ancient Romans, and my father, himself
an engineer, encouraged my enthusiasm by aiding me
to design and build model catapults and ballistae.
Some of these miniature war engines were designed to
fire arrows, others projected stone missiles. The skills
and the knowledge of these antique weapons had
never left me, and upon this occasion I had cause to
be thankful to whatever benign and foresighted di-
vinity had implanted in my youth the enthusiasm for
this hobby.

For my design I settled upon a slight modification of
the standard Roman siege catapult. The modern meaning of the word "catapult" differs from the ancient
usage. Today we think of a catapult as a curved
wooden bar, bent under pressure, which, when released, propels a stone ball held cupped at the ex-
tremity of the bar. This weapon fires up, the projectile
arcing high, to bypass a city wall and fall straight
down upon the buildings of the besieged city beyond
the wall. This design was pointless for my purposes.

The ancient siege catapult, however, was quite different. It fired an arrow or other missile horizontally
and resembled more a crossbow than what we think
of as a catapult. This design was the one I selected.
The ancient Roman catapult consisted of a sturdy
base whereon was mounted a rectangular frame. The
horizontal bottom-beam of this frame held a long

wooden trough in which the barbed missile was
lodged. This trough could be elevated or lowered by
the adjustment of a simple ratchet wheel.

This was the weapon I caused to be constructed on
the prow deck of our flying galleon.

The standard Roman catapult of this design could
fire a twenty-six-inch arrow, weighing half a pound,
and had an effective range of four hundred yards.

My modification of this design permitted the use of
a heavier arrow of forged steel weighing about six
pounds. The effective firing range was considerably
reduced, but a metal arrow was required for the simple reason that I intended to employ my projectiles
for the purpose of punching a hole through the
laminated paper hulls of enemy sky ships, to damage
their buoyancy. To this purpose I had the ironsmiths
of Shondakor laboring at their forges, making for me a
quantity of heavy steel arrows whose length and
barbed shafts made them resemble nothing less than a
sort of fantastic harpoon.

We experimented with the device and perfected
our technique. The effective range of the weapon was
about three hundred yards, which would enable us to
fire upon Zanadarian craft at a distance beyond the
range of the enemy's archery. Still, I was amazed that
the catapult could fire its harpoons to so great a distance. The mathematics simply did not work out, and
I was at a loss to explain the mystery. The simple answer may have been that the Thanatorian woods were
more resilient than their terrene equivalents or that
the tension cords I used had a far greater elasticity
than anything the ancient Romans had been able to
employ in similar weapons. Indeed this was so, for
we employed thick cords made from the "spiderwebs"
found in the jungles of the Grand Kumala.

These monster spiders were the size of small dogs.

The Ku Thad word for the species was *ximchak*. Their web strands were the thickness of heavy fishing-line and could be drawn incredibly taut without fear of snapping. From the thickness of these strands, I determined I would prefer not to encounter the spinners thereof. I have nothing in particular against insects—as witness my friendship for the arthopode, Koja—but a spider the size of a small dog is simply too much spider for my taste.

At any rate we installed our weapon and camouflaged it with a collapsible frame over which we stretched a bit of canvas. And we rested secure in the knowledge that we possessed a weapon that would prove an admirable deterrent in case we were pursued by the Sky Pirates.

It was a clear windless day when we launched forth on our venture. The Thanatorian year consists of nothing describable as seasons, so I cannot further detail the time. It may have been spring, summer, fall, or winter, for aught I could ascertain. The timelessness of life on Thanator reminds me inescapably of Edgar Rice Burroughs' descriptions of the world of Pellucidar, an imaginary region beneath the Earth's crust.

The difference lies in the fact that this gifted author imagined the inability to tell one hour or day or month from another would result in a complete ignorance of time itself and thus render his imaginary Pellucidarian natives immortally youthful.

Such was not the case on Thanator, I can assure you.

The repairs of the sky machine had taken twenty days instead of the ten promised me by Zastro.

And in that time I could swear I had aged twenty years. No Pellucidar, this jungle world of Callisto!

But at last the waiting was over and we were launched forth on our voyage into danger.

The streets and squares of Shondakor were crowded with an immense throng of citizenry, eager to witness our departure. The ornithopter was moored to an upper tier of the palace. Secured by heavy cables, it floated free on the buoyant winds. My hand-picked warrior crew was aboard and at their stations. All that remained was for us to take our final farewells.

Our captive, Ulthar, was taken aboard under heavy guard. He was a sleek-faced noble with heavy-lidded, keenly observant eyes, and a quiet demeanor that concealed, I felt certain, an active intelligence. I was also convinced that he would work ill to our cause if given the slightest opportunity.

As he mounted the gangplank under guard, Ulthar swept the deck with a thoughtful and quizzical gaze. There was a quiet smile on his lips and a gleam of ironic, mocking humor in his sharp yet sleepy-lidded eyes as he nodded a light salute to me. Then he vanished below to his locked and guarded cabin, and Yarrak repressed a growl of discontent.

"I am not easy in my mind that you are sailing into danger with a potential spy or assassin aboard, Jandar," the old man grumbled. "It seems foolhardy to the point of suicide to take that cunning, smooth-tongued snake with you on such a venture."

I shrugged. "I have taken every precaution against the possibility that he might work us harm," I reassured him. "For one thing, I have his oath of honor that he will remain our prisoner and will interfere in no way with the safety or the operation of the galleon."

"His oath of honor, eh?" Yarrak spat, as if the words had left a vile taste on his tongue. "I would not entrust my safety to the honor of a Sky Pirate! The only

Zanadarian that a man can safely trust is a dead Zan-adarian. I hope you know what you are doing, but, somehow, I doubt it!" he concluded in a troubled tone, shaking his head dubiously.

I strove to reassure him, but, to tell the truth, I was none too easy in my own mind as to the wisdom of in-cluding a potential traitor among our crew. Ulthar had gracefully yielded me his parole and his oath of honor to work us no ill, so long as we did not insist on his betrayal of any of the secrets of his countrymen; and he was a gentleman. Yet it was a risky thing, to trust an enemy at his word.

Nonetheless, it seemed worth the risk to have him with us. And I said as much to Yarrak, stressing the safety measures I had taken. Lord Yarrak and the sev-eral notables and officials of the court of Shondakor had come, arrayed in all their regal finery, to salute our departure and to offer their heartfelt good wishes on the success of our dangerous mission. Now they wished us well in our venture, praying that our mis-sion should be crowned with every success, and that we should return from our dangerous endeavor safely, bearing with us our beloved princess.

We thanked them soberly and without further ado returned their salutes, accepted the plaudits of the vast throng clustered in the streets below and lining the rooftops and the balconies of adjoining buildings, turned and mounted the gangplank to the deck of our vessel, which we had renamed the *Jalathadar*.

The term, rendered from the universal tongue spoken across the entire breadth of Thanator, signi-fies "the desperate venture" in English. And not one of us who were to serve aboard her but doubted the aptness of her new name.

My comrades took their stations.

The gangplank was detached and swung aboard and made fast, while I mounted by a succession of stairways to the openwork control cupola from which I could oversee the entire operation of the aerial galleon.

The commands were given and were relayed from station to station. The mooring lines were cast off. The deck swung giddily beneath our feet. The broad wings were extended to their fullest capacity and caught the fresh morning winds, and we swung our prow away from the towering palace. Rooftops moved beneath our keel as rapid strokes of the jointed vans drove us aloft.

Within moments we were above the tallest tower of Shondakor, and our voyage into danger had begun.

Chapter 3

ABOVE THE CLOUDS

Thrice the *Jalathadar* circled the stone-walled city of the Ku Thad, gaining altitude with each swing around the city. The streets shrank below us—the palaces and mansions and citadels of Shondakor dwindled. The mighty throng became a many-colored carpet filling the squares and rooftops. We could see the glittering curve of the great river that flows by Shondakor, and from our ever-growing height the dark mass of foliage that was the immense jungled tract of the Grand Kumala became dimly visible on the horizon.

When we had ascended to the height of about half a mile, I gave the appropriate commands. The galleon leveled off and pointed her ornate prow north and west, in the general direction of the mountain country wherein Zanadar rears her castled crest. The wheel gangs settled down to a steady rhythm, the huge vans beating slowly, the enormous rudder holding the ship of the skies steady on her course.

I leaned against the carven rail, staring down at the broad meadows that slowly passed by far underneath our keel. Soon we would be beyond the measureless plains and flying above the great jungles where I had first encountered the woman I had come at last to love.

The air was crisp and cold at this height, the wind fresh and steady. The daylight was clear and brilliant, if sourceless; the entire dome of the sky one vast dome of golden mist.

For the ten-thousandth time I wondered at the strange quirk of fate that had given unto me, of all the men of my distant world, so strange and remarkable a destiny. What inscrutable force had plucked me from amongst the millions of my faraway earth, had hurled me across the star-strewn immensities of infinite space, to this weird and savagely beautiful world of numberless marvels, to fare and battle against curious foes and terrible monsters for the heart of a beautiful and alien princess?

Was I the darling—or the plaything—of the gods?

Would I ever come to know for certain if it had been mere blind chance or the action of some unknown and superior intelligence that had transported me from my distant homeworld to this strange and wondrous world of Thanator?

Ah, well—did it really matter to me, the knowing of the answer to the mystery? Back on my distant Earth

I had been but one man among countless millions, lost in the crowd, a faceless nonentity. Here on the jungle-clad surface of mysterious Callisto I had become a princeling and a hero. Here fate or accident or chance or blind luck had thrust me into a role of transcendent importance. Here I had somehow attained to the eminence of a savior of nations. Here I had risen to a place of prominence among the great and the famous, with a voice in the destiny of great empires. Here I had found stout friends and gallant comrades and foemen worthy of my strength. And the love of a passionate and magnificent woman.

Could any man ask for more than had been thrust upon me?

The answer to the riddle meant nothing, seen in such light. I was thankful for the opportunity afforded me by the inscrutable twists and turns of fate. I had found tasks to which I was equal, burdens comparable to my strength, and a destiny glorious enough for all my ambitions.

Here on Thanator I had found the life that had never been mine back on the earth.

Here, on this mysterious and alien world, I had come home.

For hours the mighty galleon plied the skies above the trackless leagues of the Grand Kumala. We had reached an altitude considerably higher than the levels at which the ornithopters of Zanadar are accustomed by habit and tradition to fly. This was merely a precaution against any chance encounter with another of the aerial galleons of the Sky Pirates. Such an encounter would be dangerous and premature, and scouts aloft in the rigging kept careful watch against just such an eventuality.

Here we were safe from any danger. Below us, the

jungle depths were rendered hideous by prowling and nightmarish predators. I had encountered more than a few of the amazing monsters that hunt in the thick gloom of the dense jungles. It was amusing to contemplate the jungle hell beneath us, while we sailed the empty skies in thorough safety. There in the shade of those curious Thanatorian black-and-scarlet trees, we should even now be fighting for our very lives against the fanged jaws of ferocious predators. But here, in the brilliant skies of Callisto, we sailed an untroubled sea of air, alone in the windy immensities.

After an hour or so, I turned over my command to the deck officer and descended to the deck where I found Koja and the old swordmaster Lukor. I hailed them as I approached.

"Well, so far so good, Jandar!" the old Ganatolian remarked. "If our voyage continues as serenely as it has begun, we should be above the towers of Zanadar in mere days and ready for the supreme contest!"

I grinned at his sparkling eyes and ruddy cheeks. The gallant old gamecock was in fine fettle and spoiling for a fight. For all his lean shanks and silvery hair, Lukor of Ganatol was young at heart—and the greatest swordsman I had ever known. I pitied the hapless opponent who crossed blades with him, thinking him an old man: with steel in his hand, Lukor could outfight half a dozen men with only half his years.

Koja surveyed the peppery little Ganatolian expressionlessly. His solemn voice was devoid of inflection.

"Best conserve your spirit, friend Lukor," the gaunt arthopode advised humorlessly. "The contest will be upon us soon enough, and we shall need every drop of fighting courage when we are pitted against the whole of the sky navy of Zanadar—one ship against a thousand remorseless foes!"

I interrupted. "That reminds me, Koja. It still lacks

over an hour before the midday meal—time enough to practice our still unsteady skills at aerial maneuvers. As Koja says, we shall need every advantage we can summon when the chips are down, Lukor, so . . . gentlemen, to your posts!"

For an hour we put the *Jalathadar* through her paces—rising, descending, circling to port and to starboard, advancing at the three rates of speed for which the aerial contrivance had been designed, and testing our skills with the Roman catapult. This last, our "secret weapon," was the province of my friend Valkar. He had been put in charge of training a crew to man the giant crossbow, and for days he had sweated over the obstinate device until he had mastered every eccentricity of its function and operation. When the time came at last, and we faced a hostile galleon of the skies which flew the colors of Zanadar, it was the crossbow alone would prove our salvation and our ace in the hole. I wanted to be thoroughly certain the crew had mastered the new weapon, for our very lives could well depend on their facility with it.

However, we could not dare risk expending our precious store of steel darts on empty air. Once we had exhausted our supplies of the barbed bolts, the crossbow would be useless to us. And yet constant practice in aiming and firing the weapon in all winds and weathers was a prerequisite of our employment of the weapon in battle. Therefore I had bade the crewmen affix a light strand of the woven *ximchak* silk to the shaft of their practice arrows, so that once fired, they could be recovered without possibility of loss. The strand was made secure to the stout railing of the crossbow deck, and in this manner we ensured continuous and extensive weapon practice without depleting our copious but hardly inexhaustible supply of bolts.

By noon the crew was sweating but grinning happily, for the crossbow operated perfectly. With a few more such practice sessions we could gamble the safety of our persons and the success of our mission upon the abilities of Valkar's crossbowmen to employ their novel weapon against the flying ships of the City in the Clouds. We trooped down to the galley with a real appetite, and the rest of the afternoon passed without incident.

Perhaps I should include at this point some description of the extraordinary aerial contrivances that are the supreme achievement of the unique Zanadarian genius. To the eye, these flying machines resemble nothing so much as ornate, fantastical galleons left over from the Spanish Armada—galleons somehow outfitted with gigantic, flapping, batlike wings.

Technically, with an eye to naval terminology, the *Jalathadar* was a frigate and belonged to the same class of sky-going shipping as the *Kajazell*, the flying ship on which Koja and I, many months before, had served our apprenticeships at the wheels. Like a regular, sea-going frigate, the *Jalathadar* was a light, maneuverable, very speedy scout vessel built very high in poop and forecastle, the forecastle rising to about forty feet above keel level and the poop or sterncastle to some thirty-five feet, presenting the side-on appearance of a crescent moon.

The upper works of the forecastle bulged sharply in an exposed belvedere with wide, high windows which gave a good view on all three sides. There was a flat, balustraded observation deck on top of this belvedere, which served as pilot house and from which the frigate was controlled and navigated. We call this part of the ship the control cupola. A bowsprit protruded from the fore of the observation deck just above the curved row of windows of the control cupola, with an elaborately carved figurehead set at the base of the bowsprit, depicting a swaggering, bearded corsair with batlike wings and bird claws, clutching a cutlass in one hand and a jeweled crown in the other.

Farther down the curve of the hull, beneath the control cupola, at what would be the water level, if this were truly an ocean-faring vessel, two observation balconies bulged from the hull, one to either side. The sterncastle was outfitted with a similar belvedere, pointing aft, and a vertical rudderlike fin, ribbed like a gigantic Chinese fan, was attached to its rudder-stock immediately below this aft belvedere. The rud-derstock was connected to the sternpost and thence to the rear steering gear.

An immense hinged wing thrust to either side of the hull, from just below the midship-deck level. Fully extended, these wings measured one hundred and twenty-nine feet from wingtip to wingtip. The por-tions of either wing fastened directly to the hull were fixed and rigid and one with the framework; but about a third of the way out from the hull, the wings or vans were hinged in a most complex and ingenious manner, with huge pulleys and guy stays which per-mitted the crew to manipulate the outboard wing-sections so that they actually flapped up and down as do bird wings. This flapping motion is powered and controlled from mechanisms in the midship deck, the "wheel deck," as it is called. Here are located the great hand-driven wheels which communicate motion through a sequence of cogwheels—pinion wheels suc-cessively engaging ever larger cogs—the whole con-necting with the guy stays, which were thin and strong and unbelievably tough—tougher, I think, than nylon cords.

There was a simple ratchet-and-pawl arrangement on the wheels which prevented any sudden reversal; else, a contrary gust of wind might have stripped the gears, with disastrous results. These guy stays were wound about gigantic winches, set high in the upper works of the wheel deck, and the stays communicated from deck winch to wing section through rows of circular ports which ran the length of the hull just above the fixed and rigid portions of the vans.

It would have been physically impossible for such huge, cumbersome craft to fly had they not been constructed of *paper*.

The specially treated paper consisted of enormous sheets of strong papyrus, made of woven reeds beaten flat, soaked in glue, stretched over hollow plaster forms, layer upon layer, and then baked dry in brick ovens and stripped from their forms, resulting in something very like sections of light, tough, molded plastic. The oven-baked, glue-impregnated paper hulls are tough, strong, durable, and lighter than balsa wood.

In addition, every opportunity to lighten the sheer weight of the craft had been assiduously followed through. Keel, beams, masts, sternpost, stempost, bowsprit, van ribs, and so on, were mere hollow tubes. Even the figurehead was merely a hollow paper-mold. As for the outboard wing-sections, the part of the wings which flapped up and down, they were constructed on the model of bat wings, with narrow paper tubes like unsegmented bamboo rods splayed out from a center rib. Silk webbing, tightly stretched and pegged like drumheads and soaked in wax for extreme stiffness, was stretched between the ribs.

Even considering the lightweight paper construction, and all other measures taken toward conservation of weight, the sky ships would still not have been able to fly had it not been for the gas compartments. The entire bilge and lower deck was pumped full of the buoyant natural gas much like helium or hydrogen, which also filled the hollow spaces between the double hull. This natural gas, geysers of which were found among the White Mountains where the Sky Pirates dwelt, was pumped into the hollow decks and hull under high pressure, and the nozzles were then unscrewed and detached from the input hoses, which transformed them, by the addition of a simple snap-on valve, to pressure cocks, permitting some of the buoyant gas to be ejected at need so that the ship could sink to a lower level when required to do so.

Once the bilge and hollow hull were pumped full of gas, they were sealed off and calked until airtight.

The frigate had two masts amidships, set side by side, rather than fore and aft, as on a schooner. Light shrouds, stretched from mast to mast, and thence to bowsprit and sterncastle, permitted the display of signal pennants and ensign. The mastheads also were fitted with observation cupolas.

Such frigates as the *Jalathadar* had a crew strength of thirty-five officers and men, and a company of eighty wheel men, organized in eight gangs of ten men each, serving on staggered watches.

The *Jalathadar* measured eighty-five feet long. Very broad in the beam and flat-bottomed, it was almost completely weightless, and could attain a speed that might seem surprising. The average cruising speed of such a ship, with a full complement of men and supplies aboard, was such as to permit us to voyage on an average of three hundred miles per day. With a strong tailwind, that cruising speed could easily be doubled, since, unlike sea-going vessels, our prow cut empty air, not waves of heavy water, and we were as light as a balloon. When you consider that speed is attained by muscle power alone, you can begin to appreciate what a marvel of ingenuity the *Jalathadar* and her sister ships represented.

Koja and I had once been slaves, lashed to the wheels that powered the movable wingtips that propelled the aerial vehicles of Zanadar through the skies, and we were thoroughly acquainted with the backbreaking labor that task entailed.

The wheel gangs aboard the *Jalathadar,* of course, were not composed of slaves but of free men, fighting men of Shondakor. Indeed, scions of the noblest houses and princes of the highest birth manned the wheels of the galleon, for gentlemen warriors whose lineage could boast the bluest blood in the kingdom had contended jealously for a place in our crew. Thus we could hardly drive these highborn adventurers like lowly wheel slaves, groveling beneath the lash.

Fortunately, however, the *Jalathadar* did not require the motive power supplied by the wheel gangs to maintain her progress through the golden skies of Thanator. Steady prevailing winds blew from south to north across the Grand Kumala and the mountain country beyond, and the weightless corsair of the skies could ride before these gale-strength aerial tides while the wheel gangs rested. So, having achieved the upper levels at which the airstreams rushed northwards, the wheel gangs were released from their labors to join us in the galley, and were then liberated from further toil to stroll about the several decks, enjoying the splendors of the view.

Riding a strong tailwind, we passed the first day's voyage without incident, making more than three hundred and twenty miles before nightfall and employing the strength of the wheel gangs only at certain intervals.

During the night, we reduced speed to lessen the possibility of straying from our course, for such aerial travel upon the Jungle Moon affords certain navigational hazards unique to Callisto.

But I shall soon have reason to discuss these problems, and will pass over them here.

The second day of our voyage dawned bright and clear, and I rose from my bunk, breakfasted lightly in my cabin, and went forth to the deck, ascending to the pilot house (or control cupola, as I should call it) to check the night log. We were on course, with a strong but steady tailwind. Glancing through the broad observation windows, I saw the trackless leagues of the Grand Kumala reeling away far below our keel, and once again reflected philosophically on the fact that those jungle paths beneath us were aprowl with ferocious yathrib and savage deltagar and other monstrous predators, while here aloft in a cloudless sky we floated across the world in utter safety.

Toward late afternoon of the second day our tailwind increased and began to pose a problem. It first became apparent when a deck officer called to my attention that the Kumala below was now hidden behind thick clouds, greatly reducing our visibility. At the extreme height at which the *Jalathadar* now rode the winds, we were actually above the clouds and could enjoy the queer experience of *looking down* at a cloudy sky.

Cloud formations are rather rare on Thanator, or, to be precise, are seldom particularly visible, at least from the land surface of the Jungle Moon. The reason for this lack of visibility is that the skies themselves are composed of curious golden vapors, uniformly illuminated from horizon to horizon, and against this hazy dome of golden light what clouds there are, are very difficult to see. But from our present height, clouds completely obscured the jungle country below from our view. From horizon to horizon the land below was concealed behind a thick blanket of milky vapor. The sight was curious and novel, but seemed to present no particular hazards.

Somewhat later, however, the duty officer summoned me to the control cupola. This particular officer was a nobly born gentleman of high Ku Thad rank named Haakon. He was a tall, sturdily built, serious-faced man in his forties, steady, strong, reliable, with the rare ability to keep his head in a crisis. He saluted me gravely as I entered the cupola and called to my attention yet again the dense blanket of clouds which obscured the lands below from our vision.

"I have already observed the cloud formations," I said easily, "and, since we do not have any reason to descend to a lower altitude for some time, can see no problem."

"The problem, sir, is one of navigation," he said simply.

I understood his meaning at once, and cursed myself for not realizing sooner the hazard our current lack of visibility presented, for navigation through the skies of Thanator is a problem doubtless unique to this world.

You will understand what I mean when you consider that the sun of our solar system is too greatly distant from Callisto to be particularly visible, save as one of the more brilliant stars. On Earth, navigation by means of solar observations is the simplest of feats; the sun rises in the east, traverses the dome of the sky, and sets in the west; hence, at any given hour of the day one can at least ascertain the cardinal directions in general at a glance.

Not so on Thanator. As well, the heavens of the Jungle Moon are thickly obscured by crawling golden vapors, as I have remarked earlier; hence, navigation by study of the fixed stars or constellations is also virtually impossible.

True, the larger of Callisto's sister moons of Jupiter are visible orbs of colored light during the hours of darkness, but even here a problem imposes itself. For the Jovian moons, at least the larger ones, circumnavigate their primary in a system or orbits of bewildering complexity. It is a mathematical problem of truly staggering difficulties, attempting to navigate the skies of Thanator at night, guided only by the positions of the moons of Jupiter.

"I see what you mean, Haakon," I said ruefully. "But let us not worry about problems that may soon correct themselves unaided. The cloud zone may soon break up, and the clouds disperse, permitting us to obtain clear visibility of the land below."

"Perhaps, sir, but perhaps not," Haakon gravely remarked. "But if so, it must occur very soon, or it will do us no good at all. For night is almost upon us."

I should perhaps explain here that the peculiar and inexplicable illumination of the golden vapor that fills the skies of Callisto ceases with startling unanimity at nightfall. On Earth the solar orb declines gradually into sunset, twilight and afterglow, but on Callisto, when day ends, the transition is one of surprising suddenness. One moment the Jungle Moon is bathed in ubiquitous golden radiance—the next, it is plunged into total darkness. Hence, unless the clouds broke very soon, so that we could obtain clear sightings of major landmarks by which to correct our course and orient our flight, the eventual dispersal of the vapors would do no good at all.

"Well," I said, "let us hope our course is undeviating." The grizzled senior officer shook his head reluctantly.

"We have been meeting a slight but definite headwind for the past hour or two," he confessed. "I have been compensating for it more or less by pure guesswork, but if we must fly blind during the entire night, compensating against this headwind, our course by morning may have been deflected off true northwest by a wide margin. If only, sir, we had the assistance of an experienced pilot. But I assume our prisoner remains obdurately uncooperative?"

I nodded. Captain Ulthar had steadfastly refused to lend us any assistance whatsoever. Bidding Haakon to continue compensating for the headwind and to summon me to the cupola should there be any change at all in the weather conditions, I descended by the circular stair into the captain's cabin to consult the Zanadarian navigational guides. I did not expect these to be of any real help, nor were they.

Lacking sun or moon or stars, navigation through the skies of Thanator is a highly complex art. The Sky Pirates who command the aerial vessels are seasoned and experienced veterans and doubtless know the winds and ways of the Thanatorian heavens from past familiarity. However, the galleon's cabin was supplied with certain standard guides, among which was a sort of sky atlas which charted the major prevailing winds which were bewilderingly complicated beyond the abilities of a mere novice to quickly master. I puzzled over the atlas but could make nothing of its cryptic notations. The guidebooks also included an ephemeris of the orbits of the visible moons of Jupiter, but these also were exceedingly complex. True, they charted the variations in the lunar positions and related these to the cardinal directions, but the variations were minute and intertwined, and, lacking a compass—an invention for which the Thanatorians seem to lack reason to develop—we would, it seemed, be flying blind during the hours of darkness.

There was really nothing we could do about this. Difficulties in navigation were among the several unknown factors we had risked in attempting this voyage into the unknown. Ostensibly, it had seemed remarkably simple to traverse the land surface of Callisto between Shondakor and Zanadar. The City in the Clouds lies north by northwest of the realm of the Ku Thad, and it would seem an easy task to fly thither. You pass the plains, traverse the Grand Kumala, enter the northerly mountain country, and simply look about for the mountaintop city of the Sky Pirates. Nothing could have been simpler, or so it seemed at the beginning.

Night fell without a break in the cloud blanket. We flew on into darkness, still battling against an unsteady headwind that pushed against our prow and strove in uneven gusts to drive us east.

At the captain's table, over dinner that evening, our navigational difficulties were the central topic of discussion. Our captive, Ulthar, who ate with us, being an officer of noble birth, smiled gently when peppery old Lukor loudly and pointedly suggested he might place his knowledge and experience at our service.

"I am certain the gentleman of Ganatol would not seriously suggest violating the terms under which I have given Captain Jandar my parole," he said mockingly. "The nobly born gentleman will recall that our agreement does not include my revealing the secrets of my people, among which the art of aerial navigation must surely be numbered."

Lukor screwed up his face in an expression of disgust.

"I had assumed the nobly born gentleman of Zanadar would have yielded to reason," he said acerbically, "if only since to keep silence in this danger imperils his life as well as ours!"

Ulthar laughed quietly, and turned hooded, mocking eyes upon me. "It would seem, Captain Jandar, that my faith in your exceptional abilities is greater than that of those you are pleased to call your friends. For, unlike them, I have no fears that you will prove unable to meet this present minor emergency."

Lukor growled a colorful oath and addressed himself to his plate. Ulthar remained quiet but observant throughout the remainder of the meal.

The cabin lamp swayed on its creaking chain as the great galleon of the skies trembled to the buffets of the tailwind. Wine sloshed in our goblets; plates slid to and fro on the table.

We ate in silence, each busied with his own thoughts. My own were far off in the mountaintop citadel of our foes, the remorseless and rapacious Sky Pirates of Zanadar. I wondered how my beloved Darloona fared at this hour. Had she given over all hope of rescue by now?

The meal finished, we each sought our bunks and uneasy and troubled slumbers. All that night we flew on into mystery, wondering where dawn would find us.

We awoke in an unknown world.

Book II

OFF THE MAP

Chapter 4

THE UNKNOWN SEA

Before dawn I arose from a night of broken and uneasy slumbers, through which I had tossed and turned continuously, my rest disturbed and troubled by ominous dreams.

Rising from my bunk, I hastily threw on my wide-sleeved white blouse, thigh-length leather tunic, calf-high boots and cloak, girdle, and sword-belt, and went up on deck to observe the sudden miracle of daybreak on Thanator.

The reader can, I am sure, envision the extent of my distress as I looked over the side upon an unknown portion of the surface of Thanator.

The swift, brilliant dawn had illuminated the world from horizon to horizon, banishing the darkness that had long enshrouded the surface of the Jungle Moon.

By daylight it could be seen that the cloud blanket had indeed broken at last, but only recently, for still our vision of the world below was obscured by the whitish haze of extensive vapors, although these were in the process of dispersal. The layer of clouds had parted, here and there, revealing broken glimpses of the land surface. And my heart sank with dismay, for I could see nowhere the heavy jungles of the Grand Kumala that should have been beneath our keel; neither, raising my head toward what I fancied was the north, could I see anything resembling the mountain country on the horizon ahead.

The White Mountains of Varan-Hkor are the mightiest range upon all of Thanator* and should have been dimly visible on the northern horizon by this second day of our flight. But mountains were nowhere in sight.

Instead, the breaks in the cloud blanket below revealed rolling hills, broad meadows, uncultivated fields, and, far off to what seemed to be the east, a city or town.

I climbed into the control cupola, exchanged terse greetings with the officer of the watch, and consulted the night log. The slight headwind which had deflected us from our course had, it seemed, continued all night long, blowing first from the portside and later from the starboard. Each time the headwind had changed direction the watch officer had compensated by altering the pitch of our rudder and ailerons slightly, using his own untutored judgment as to the degree of compensation required to keep us on our north-by-northwest course.

Toward dawn the headwind had changed yet again, and this time it blew at gale strength, forcing the watch officer to lift the ship a few hundred feet to an even higher altitude than that to which we had held during the earlier portions of the night. By thus rising

---

* By this, Captain Dark means the *known portions* of Thanator. For some unexplained reason, the inhabitants of Shondakor and the other civilized races Captain Dark has encountered thus far in his adventures, are acquainted only with that hemisphere of Callisto which is perpetually turned towards its primary, the planet Jupiter. Nothing seems to be known concerning the "dark side" of the moon, or, at any rate, very little.—L.C.

above the strong headwind, he had diminished the
degree whereby we were being deflected from our
course, but he had lifted the *Jalathadar* into an air-
stream moving at greater velocity than the prevailing
air current we had been riding.

In other words, we were farther along than we
should have been, and our course had probably been
deflected to a considerable extent. But had we strayed
off course to the east or to the west? There seemed no
way of telling for certain.

I strained my eyes to make out the details of the
city that was just visible on the horizon. It lay amid a
level plain, so it certainly could not be Zanadar. If we
had diverged due east, at right angles from our desired course, we might be approaching the home city
of Lukor the Swordmaster, although it seemed highly
unlikely that we had come so far as to approach the
outskirts of Ganatol.

On the other hand, the fickle winds might have
blown us off course to the west. Since we were obviously well beyond the jungles of the Grand Kumala,
that would place us on the remote margin of the
known hemisphere of Thanator. For the area due
west of the northernmost edge of the Grand Kumala
is commonly left blank on all Thanatorian maps I
have ever seen.

If that was the case, then we were flying toward an
unknown city, approaching the margins of the hemisphere itself.

I turned, calling over one of the cupola crew, and
sent him below decks with instructions to rouse Master
Lukor from his bed and, ere long, the old swordmaster joined me in the cupola, yawning and grum-
bling and rubbing the slumber from his eyes.

I directed his attention to the foreign city, which

by now was clearly visible on the horizon, although the regions beyond and about it were still hidden beneath an impenetrable layer of clouds. I inquired if the city could be Ganatol; he replied quite firmly in the negative.

"Not a chance of it, lad," he said. "Ganatol is built on the shores of the River Iquon, and you can clearly see there is no river about yonder town."

I mused over the charts.

"It hardly seems possible we could have gone farther than Ganatol," I said. "But beyond Ganatol lies the city of Narouk, on the shores of the Corund Laj. Could that possibly be Narouk, do you think?"

He chewed his lower lip, fiercely eyeing the distant buildings.

"Well, I have visited Narouk in my time, but I cannot say as how I am so intimately acquainted with the city as to instantly recognize it from the air. However, if that is Narouk, then where is the Corund Laj, my boy?"

"Still hidden beneath the cloudbanks, perhaps," I hazarded. He shrugged, obviously uncertain. And indeed it did seem highly unlikely that we could possibly have traveled such a great distance during the night—unless our wind had increased very considerably, which was not at all impossible, and could well have gone unnoticed, due to our unfamiliarity with the Zanadarian techniques of measuring wind velocity.

The Corund Laj, I should perhaps explain, is a great freshwater inland sea, the nearest thing to an ocean that is to be found upon the surface of Callisto. Callisto's surface is one continuous extent of dry land, broken only by two bodies of water. The smaller of these, which is called the Sanmur Laj, or the Lesser Sea, is located far south and west of the Plains of Haratha, where the Yathoon Horde rules the grasslands below the Grand Kumala, stretching, I assume, to the unexplored regions of the south pole.

The larger of the twin seas of Callisto is called the Corund Laj, or the Greater Sea, and it occupies the extreme northeastern portion of Thanatorian maps. It is the center of a maritime civilization that has little contact with Shondakor and boasts of several powerful cities, of which Narouk and easterly Soraba are among the less prominent. Farz, on the ultimate northern coast of the Corund Laj, is the northernmost of all the cities of Thanator, and directly in our path, if indeed we had diverged in an easterly direction.

But the city visible to us could not possibly be Farz. It was most likely Narouk.

An hour or two of steady flying brought us within the vicinity of the unknown city, and by that point we became convinced it was indeed Narouk. For the clouds encircling the mysterious walled town had broken at last, dispersing before the uneven gusts of a freshening morning wind. And beyond the city could now be clearly seen the glittering waters of a considerable expanse of sea that could only be the Corund Laj.

Now that we could be more or less certain about our position, and knew the extent to which we had been blown off course during the night, we could orient ourselves. To reach Zanadar we now had to fly due west, traversing the entirety of the White Mountains. This would add considerably to the length of our voyage, which was no short distance anyway. As the crow flies, the distance from Golden Shondakor to the mountaintop fortress-city of the Sky Pirates was some 310 *korads*—or twenty-two hundred miles, more or less, in Earth measurement. Due to the shifting headwinds, we had diverged off course by about seventy-five *korads* during the night.

In other words, to continue our voyage to Zanadar was possible, but our inadvertent detour had added something like five hundred miles to the distance we had to travel.

We discussed the new course in the control cupola.

The officer in charge of stores, a young noble named Amthar, shook his head doubtfully.

"We do not have a sufficient supply of drinking water for so great an additional distance," he said. I nodded—weight is a vital factor in the operation of the flying galleons of Zanadar, and our stores of foodstuffs and drinkables had been calculated to the last ounce before we left the city of the Ku Thad.

"Nor can we count on finding mountain lakes or springs, once we have entered the White Mountains," Amthar pointed out. "The territory is under the domination of the Sky Pirates, and our charts of the mountain country are but cursory."

"Surely, gentlemen, restocking your water supply should afford you no problem, since we are approaching the shores of the Corund Laj," a suave voice commented. I glanced up, more than a little surprised, for it was our Zanadarian captive, Ulthar, who had contributed this suggestion. He generally kept aloof from our councils, and had thus far been careful to avoid making any contributions to our discussions. Why he had volunteered a helpful comment on this problem I could not hazard a guess. However, his suggestion was a simple one of pointing out the obvious—for, as I have already remarked, the navigable waterways of Thanator, including her two immense landlocked seas, are composed of fresh water—so I dismissed my instant suspicions and did not give him any further thought.

We decided to come down over the Corund Laj and take on fresh supplies of water sufficient to carry us the additional distance we must travel. There was no particular hazard involved in doing this, for we were not likely to encounter another aerial vessel of the Sky Pirates in this part of the world, and although the folk of Narouk and the other Perushtarian cities about the shores of the Corund Laj were the avowed foes of Zanadar, we could easily avoid descending in the vicinity of the cities and elude any risk of trouble without much problem. And thus we resolved.

By late morning we were well out over the Corund Laj. It glittered below us like an immense shield of hammered brass, dented by shallow waves, mirroring the golden splendor of the daylit sky. We had circled around Narouk to avoid discovery, and made our descent over the open sea.

It was not, of course, necessary for the *Jalathadar* to actually make a landing on the waters in order to take on fresh supplies. The flying galleons are not meant to land and might well break up from their own cumbersome dimensions if they ever came to rest on the land surface of the Jungle Moon. In Zanadar they are more or less permanently aloft, although securely tethered to mooring masts, and only come to rest when they are in urgent need of repair and then only in special dock-facilities designed to deal with their fragile structure.

We brought the aerial vessel down so that her keel floated only twenty yards above the rippling waves. At that point, holding her as steady as possible, waxed waterbags were lowered over the side on long lines. They were dipped into the sparkling waves and teams of crew members hauled them up, full to overflowing, to the deck again. It was a slow and time-consuming process, but easy enough.

I was lounging idly against the deck rail, watching the men dragging up the waterbags, without a thought of danger in my mind. Our captive, Ulthar, came sauntering over to where I leaned against the rail and engaged me in casual conversation. I thought nothing of this, and certainly had no reason to suspect the smooth-tongued Zanadarian of any ulterior motive, although I did not like Ulthar or enjoy his company. But he had been given the freedom of the deck, and had, in fact, the run of the ship, except for certain key areas, such as the wheel room or the signal cabin, where he might just possibly have injured our mission through a bit of adroit sabotage. I did not really trust the Sky Pirate, although I must confess he had thus far given me not the slightest reason to regret my decision to bring him along.

By a little after noon the last waterbags had been drawn aboard, dripping and full. The duty officer in the forward control cupola, receiving the signal from the deck officer, gave the command to come about and go aloft. With an immense creaking groan the enormous jointed wing-flaps began their ponderous motions, sending booming gusts across the deck, drowning out Ulthar's soft tones. We were ascending rapidly now, and I waved him to silence, as it was not possible to continue our conversation over the slow, steady beat of the huge wings.

He nodded, understanding, and half-turned away as if to leave the deck. Then he glanced out over the waters of the sea, now rapidly dwindling beneath our keel, and his eyes widened with amazement and disbelief. He gave voice to an involuntary cry of surprise, and, as I turned to see what it was that he had seen which had so startled him, Ulthar acted.

He had chosen the perfect moment to strike. While one or two men were still on the deck, none of them were anywhere near us and no one was looking in our direction. I had turned away to search sea and sky for whatever it was that he had seen, and thus my back was to him. As swiftly and unobtrusively as if he had carefully rehearsed the act—which he may well have done, in the privacy of his quarters, for all I know—he bent swiftly, caught me about the waist, kicked my legs out from under me, and, rising, *threw me over the side!*

It was done so swiftly and smoothly, that before I even knew what was happening, I was falling through the air.

There was no time to catch hold of anything, to cry out—and I fell like a stone.

I had a confused vision of sea and sky wheeling giddily about as I fell. There was one fleeting glimpse of the *Jalathadar* above me—an enormous, dark-winged shape, blotting out the sky.

And the next instant I struck the waves of the Corund Laj with the force of a battering ram.

The impact knocked the air out of my lungs. I sank under the blue waves in a rush of foaming bubbles, half-conscious, stunned, gasping for air. I would doubtless have drowned in my semiconscious state, had not the shock of plunging so precipitously beneath the icy waters brought me to consciousness again.

With that hair-trigger instinct of self-preservation that is part of the equipment of the fighting man, I shut my lips against the icy flood, ignoring the lancing agony that blazed through me. My starved lungs cried out for air, but I clenched my jaws tight-shut with every atom of willpower I could summon.

In a wild spasm of threshing limbs, I struck out

wildly. A moment later my head broke through the waves and I treaded water mechanically, gulping delicious air into my aching lungs.

I was stunned and dazed, shaken by the unexpected calamity, but unharmed.

Far above me, all but lost against the strange gold glare of the noontide sky, the *Jalathadar* had dwindled to a minute fleck. I watched helplessly as it hovered for a moment, and then turned its prow due west in the direction of Zanadar.

In a moment it was out of sight. And I was lost, alone and helpless, amid the waters of the unknown sea.

Chapter 5

I BECOME A SLAVE

There was no time for me to indulge myself in the luxury of cursing Ulthar for his treachery. Every breath of air is a precious commodity to a man who has just narrowly escaped drowning, and not to be idly squandered on futile imprecations.

And I was not out of danger yet. The frigate had come down to take on new stores of water quite some considerable distance from shore, so as to insure against the possibility of being seen. Thus I had quite a distance to swim before I could hope to feel dry land under my feet.

I suppose I am as good a swimmer as any other man,

and, like most, I suppose I tend to think of myself as being more proficient in the art than is actually the case. In any event, I came perilously close to not reaching dry land at all. For one thing, I was still groggy from the fall from the *Jalathadar;* for another, I was fully dressed in the traditional garments of a Thanatorian fighting-man. The costume, I need hardly stress, was never designed with a lengthy swim in mind.

Thanatorian warriors generally wear high-necked, sleeveless, thigh-length tunics of supple leather over blouselike shirts and loincloths. Together with gauntlets, a heavy leathern girdle about the midsection, sometimes thickly encrusted with noble metals and precious stones, cloak, boots or buskins, sword and dagger and purse, the basic costume is common wherever the warriors of Thanator may chance to dwell. The only exception to this is among the arthopodes, the chitin-clad insect-men who roam the great Haratha plains in mighty hordes. They, of course, go devoid of any raiment save sword-belt or baldric.

As you can readily imagine, the prospect of swimming the considerable distance to shore encumbered by such garments is not a pleasant one. I tore away my cloak first, kicked off my boots, and ere long was forced to struggle out of the heavy girdle and sword-belt or be drowned. Naked save for a water-soaked leather tunic and clout, I staggered ashore, collapsing in the wet gray sand, and lay there panting and spitting up seawater for a time, before I felt able to drag myself farther up the land.

My condition was truly a desperate one. Weaponless, alone and friendless, in an alien land, my chances for survival rested upon imponderables and uncertainties. However, I did not give way to despair. Even now, my friends aboard the flying vessel might have discovered my absence, even now, they might be reversing the course of the *Jalathadar*. Within mere moments the winged shape of the frigate might loom blackly against the clear golden skies, lowering a rope ladder whereby I might regain her decks, with no worse than a wetting gained from my adventure.

Then sword steel flashed, mirror-bright, before my eyes.

I looked up, past the glittering scimitar, into a hard, unfriendly face and a pair of alert, curious, and wary eyes.

The western portion of the known hemisphere of Thanator is occupied by Corund Laj, the greater of the two seas of the Jungle Moon. This sea, and the coastlands about it, is dominated by a race of red-skinned, hairless men called Perushtarians.

Merchants, traders, shopkeepers, theirs is a mercantile civilization like ancient Carthage; culturally, however, their life style has more in common with medieval Persia. They are a league of free cities—Farz, to the north, Narouk, in the west, and Soraba, on the south coast of the Greater Sea. Their civilization is, for some reason unknown to me, called the Bright Empire, and its capital, Glorious Perusht, lies on a large island off the southern coast, which has the unique distinction of being the only isle on all of Thanator.

I have referred to the Perushtarians as being red-skinned. This conjures up a vision of the American Indians, the aboriginal denizens of the North American continent. Actually, when you stop to think of it, the term "red-skinned" is misapplied to American Indians, who are more a ruddy copper than red. The citizens of the Bright Empire of Perushtar, however, are truly red—a bright crimson, like ripe tomatoes, and (to compound the vegetable simile) equally hairless.

Although my adventures had carried me far and near across the face of mysterious Callisto, it so chanced that I had never really come into contact with the Perushtarian race. Now I found myself facing capture by one of them—and now I had the leisure to curse the treachery of Ulthar and my own temerity in stripping off my baldric and scabbard during the long, hazardous, exhausting swim to shore.

The Perushtarian who stood near me on the wet gray sands, holding the flashing scimitar in hard, capable hands, was a squat, heavy-shouldered specimen with a grim, ruthless face and questioning, uncompromising eyes.

Bald as are all of his race, he wore a fringed cap of pea-green velvet. A knee-length robe of bright blue-dyed cloth, edged with scarlet tassels, and a gaudy sash of many colors wound many times around his middle completed his most un-Thanatorian costume. Soft-soled buskins of gilt leather shod his feet. Copper armlets were clasped about his thick biceps and muscular wrists, and a dozen or so small paste amulets hung about his throat on a thin silver ring.

We stared at each other in wordless silence for a long moment, I sprawled on the water-soaked sand, he spread-legged, alert for the slightest movement on my part. From the expression on his heavy-jowled, grim-lipped face, I had no doubt he would sink that glistening, razory blade into my flesh at the first sign of any hostility from me.

Perhaps I should have sprung at him that first moment. In hindsight, it seems likely I could have scooped up a handful of wet, gritty sand—hurled it

into his eyes, blinding him—and wrested the heavy
scimitar from him with ease. But—alas!—I temporized,
I delayed. Expecting the return of the *Jalathadar* at
any moment, I did nothing whatsoever.

He stared down at me narrowly. Then, barking out
a curt name, he summoned his companion or servitor,
a fat fellow with bland, cool eyes, also hefting a heavy
steel blade.

"Gamel!" my captor barked.

"Aye, lord?"

"Come and look at what the sea has cast up at my
very feet." The second Perushtarian hove into view, to
peer down at me with bored, incurious eyes.

"Notice anything odd about him?" the first man inquired.

The underling shrugged.

"Well, he has strange coloring for a Zanadarian,"
the fat man the other had addressed as Gamel observed mildly. "I had not known, lord, they came in
such a variety of skin and hair and eyes!"

The Perushtarian laughed harshly, and I realized
then that they must have been nearby when the aerial
galleon came down to take on water. We had thought
ourselves unobserved; so, at least, we had hoped, but
now the falsity of this was revealed.

The first Perushtarian spoke to me curtly:

"You—fellow! What is your name and nation?"

"My name is Jandar," I said unperturbedly. "And my
homeland is called the United States of America."

He blinked at the unfamiliar name.

"The, the Yew-Nine-Estates," he fumbled with the
name, then shrugged, and gave it up. "Well, it must
be a far land indeed, for never before have I seen a
man with clear bronze skin and yellow hair, such as
yours."

"It is indeed very far away," I said gravely. Nor did I exaggerate. My country was, at the time, some three hundred and ninety million miles distant from the shores of the Corund Laj. "Far away" is an understatement!

"So it must be," the Perushtarian said. "For never have I heard of it, in all my days. Do all men there have skin and hair of such strange colors as your own?"

"We come," I assured him, "in a variety of colors. But we generally think alike. For example, few of us enjoy lying full length on wet sand with a sword held at our throats."

He laughed at that, and stepped back, motioning me to rise. I got to my feet, wiping the wet muddy sand from my garments as best I might, stealing a searching glance aloft for some sign of the *Jalathadar*. But the skies were clear! Surely, by now, my friends must have missed me, must have had sufficient time to search the galleon from rudder to figurehead, finding me inexplicably missing.

The fat man, Gamel, shrewdly noted my surreptitious glance skyward.

"The slave supposes his comrades may discover his absence and return in search of him, lord," he pointed out.

The other nodded.

"Then let us be on our way. Secure him, Gamel," he growled curtly. Then, turning on his heel, and giving me no further attention, he strode up the beach. I now observed a sizable caravan waiting on the high ground. And my heart sank within me, for with every passing moment my hopes of rescue became slimmer.

Gamel forced me to kneel, threatening me with his blade. With swift, sure hands he lashed my wrists together behind my back and settled a sort of halter around my neck, by which he led me up the beach to a pack-thaptor, securing my neck line to the harness of the beast.

"Slave, you are now the property of the lord Cham of Narouk, of the House of Iskelion," he said, mounting the saddle of his beast.

Before I could speak he touched the flanks of his steed with a braided quirt, and the caravan lurched into motion. I had not been ready for the sudden motion and was flung headlong in the dust. I would have been dragged to my death by the thaptor had I not managed to struggle to my feet.

Thus, running along behind a pack-thaptor in the caravan of Cham the merchant, I came to the city of Narouk.

As a nameless, helpless slave!

Thaptors are large, wingless birds of a species unknown upon my native world, but not unlike the terrene ostrich—if you can imagine a four-legged ostrich as large as a horse.

A thaptor is as large as a stallion, with an arched neck and four legs, but there its dim resemblance to the equine species terminates. For the creatures have clawed feet, spurred like roosters, and a stiff ruff of feathers around the base of their skulls, not unlike the ruff of a vulture. They have sharp, curved, yellow, parrotlike beaks, glaring eyes with black irises and brilliant orange pupils. In the wild, they are savage predators—even man-eaters, on occasion. Broken with great difficulty to bit and saddle, they never lose their innate ferocity and never become completely tamed, no matter with what harsh discipline they are abused.

The thaptor to whose harness I was roped was a

particularly vicious brute. It did not like having a strange man running along at its heels and did everything it could think of to discourage my following in its tracks, kicking up dust in my face and frequently spurting ahead so that it could make me fall and be dragged a bit, until heavy blows from the wooden rod borne by the caravan master beat it back into line.

What with having fallen several score yards into an ice-cold sea, having swum ashore half-unconscious, weighed down with heavy gear, swallowing about half of the waters of the Corund Laj en route, and now being forced to run several miles behind a thaptor or suffer a broken neck, I was in sorry shape by the time we reached the gates of Narouk.

My water-soaked leather tunic was now thickly coated with white road dust. My bare feet, gashed by innumerable stony shards from running over the gravel road, left tracks of blood as I limped through the city gates at the tail of the caravan. I was winded and more than half-strangled from the rope loop, tied in a hangman's knot, which Gamel had thrown around my neck. Considering all of this, it is perhaps understandable that I recall but little of my first close-up look of a Perushtarian city and nothing whatsoever of the outer walls, grounds, and gardens of the villa of Cham, my master.

I began to recover my senses in the slave pens. An old man with a worn, lined, kindly face and hands as gentle as a woman's was tenderly bathing my bloody feet and applying a soothing ointment of some kind. I remember it had the sharp, spicy, pungent odor of spruce-gum.

Someone else, a woman naked to the waist, her long black hair tied back at the nape of her neck in what I later came to recognize as a slave knot, was washing the road dust from my face and hair. With a moistened cloth, she very gently cleansed the grit from my nostrils, inner mouth, eyes, and ears. From time to time she lifted to my lips a clay pot filled with strong red wine, almost as fierce and potent as raw brandy.

I never drank anything more delicious in my life.

My tunic was in sorry shape by this time. Prolonged immersion in water had cracked and split the supple leather, and being dragged from time to time over the flinty path, when I happened to trip and fall, had not improved it, either. They stripped it from me, and the ragged, muddy loincloth as well. I don't recall whether the woman left the room during these intimate ministrations or not, nor does it matter. I was past caring, and false modesty is a luxury in a life as adventure-filled as mine.

At any rate, now that I was a slave, I no longer was entitled to a warrior's tunic, and, my bedraggled garments removed, I donned the short cotton smock of a domestic slave.

The old man, whose name was Kanelon, as I later learned, and the woman, whose name was Imarra, having completed their ministrations, fed me a hot, spicy meat-broth with chewy chunks of tough black bread swimming in it and let me stretch out on a straw pallet to sleep.

Before slumber overcame my senses, however, while I lay there deliciously at ease, wine and hot broth making me drowsy, I vaguely became aware of the two slaves discussing me.

The woman was saying something about me. I strained to make out her words, which were spoken in low tones.

"Never have I seen a man with hair and eyes of such unusual color," she was saying. "An outlander, obviously, but from what land or city?"

The old man shrugged. "I don't know. The slave master says Gamel called him a Zanadarian."

"He does not look like any Zanadarian I have ever seen," the woman commented, eyeing me dubiously.

"Perhaps he was only a Zanadarian slave. According to Gamel, he fell overboard into the sea from one of the Zanadarian flying machines. He is lucky to be alive, if that is so."

"Lucky?" the woman asked, incredulously. "Perhaps he is fortunate that he did not drown in his fall. But he is certainly not lucky to have been fished out by the lord Cham—*this month of all months!*"

The woman's peculiar remark attracted my interest, and, feigning slumber, I lay there, listening intently.

Kanelon grunted, "Aye, 'tis true. Unless he has some needed skill, 'tis certain the lord Cham will render him up for the Tribute. Poor fellow! Should that be the case, he may wish he had drowned in the waves of the Corund Laj after all."

The woman grunted.

"You pretend to knowledge no one claims for sure," she said. "After all, no one knows what happens to those poor men sent out as part of the Tribute. Mayhap they are not so badly treated."

Kanelon laughed shortly.

"No one knows what happens to Tribute slaves, because in all these years not one of them has ever come back here!" he said. "I say they are slain horribly, and my guess is as good as any—dispute me if you will, woman!"

Imarra sighed dispiritedly.

"Anyway, is it not a pity the poor man was not seized by the lords Ashulok or Farzemum, or one of the others, for upon the lord Cham this month alone falls the burden of supplying one hundred slaves to go forth from here to face an unknown doom!"

If they exchanged further words, I know it not, for weariness had whelmed my curiosity, and I fell asleep.

Chapter 6

SLAVERY IN NAROUK

During the next two days I remained a slave in the villa of the lord Cham.

I was not mistreated, but neither was I coddled. Slaves are a valuable commodity in the Bright Empire, for it is their labor that supports the landed aristocracy of the merchant princes of Perushtar. My lacerated feet healed with miraculous swiftness, due to the excellent medicinal properties in the salve with which Kanelon had anointed my cuts and bruises.

From this garrulous, trusted house slave, Kanelon, I learned much during the idleness enforced upon me by my injuries. The old man had been born into slavery and knew no other life: slavery was a natural condition, as far as he was concerned, and he had no particular desire for freedom. This may seem remarkable to my reader. It certainly seemed remarkable to me; either the poor old fellow had been so broken by his degraded status, or he was of a servile, cringing sort. I talked at length with him and discovered to my considerable surprise that neither was the case.

When I asked him why he did not desire to be free, he replied that if he were free he would have no one to feed or house or care for him. As a slave, he was an item of property in the possession of the great House of Iskelion, and it was the responsibility of the House of Iskelion to feed him, clothe him, and supply him with a place to sleep. As a free man, no one would care whether he lived or died, and no one would mind whether or not he starved to death in a cold alley some night—as would most likely be his fate, were he ever foolish enough to accept the dubious gift of freedom.

I learned from the talkative old man that the Perushtarians were an oligarchy, pure and simple. There were thirty or forty great merchant princes who held all or most of the wealth of the Bright Empire. My owner, Cham, was a younger third nephew of the fabulously wealthy and powerful Iskelion family, whose ancient wealth was primarily built upon ocean trade, import and export, and slave-raising.

If it seems somewhat curious to my reader that an oligarchy can pass as an empire, all I can say is that I was puzzled by this myself. Upon questioning old Kanelon, I learned that the great merchant houses had long ago combined into urban centers for mutual protection. Eight or ten of the great families were dominant in each of the Perushtarian cities. Here in Narouk, for example, the Houses of Iskelion, Ashlamun, Chemed, Ildth, and Sarpelio held the majority of power, while three or four minor houses scrabbled and quarreled for secondary status.

Obviously, a city as divided as Narouk would long ago have been torn asunder by civil war had not some compromise government system been worked out. The system was an admirably simple one. Each of the Perushtarian cities was ostensibly ruled by an hereditary prince called a Seraan. While the ultimate administrative authority was vested in the Seraan, he was actually powerless, for the Seraan was denied any opportunity to amass wealth, and in the Bright Empire, wealth alone was the source of power.

While the Seraan of Narouk held the Ruby Seal, whose affixture to every law or decree made each such a legal instrument, it was also denied to the Seraan to initiate legislation of any kind. All of the laws which came before the Seraan to be sealed into law originated in a sort of parliament of judges who were the representatives of the great merchant families of Narouk and whose influence, and the weight of whose vote, was reckoned in direct proportion to the wealth and prominence of the family each judge represented.

I must admit I was both astonished and amused that so blatantly oligarchic a system of government could actually work. It was like late nineteenth-century capitalism run wild. However, it did work, and, in fact, under the oligarchy, the Bright Empire of Perushtar flourished. The cities—if I may judge the whole of the empire by what I observed in the city of Narouk— were clean, handsome, gorgeously decorated with monumental art. There were no reeking slums and no beggars, because there was no poverty at all. Those who were not rich were owned or patronized by the rich, as, for example, the artisan class. And for a civilization whose energies were devoted almost entirely to the acquisition of wealth, there was a surprisingly brilliant culture. Theaters, sports arenas, and literary salons abounded. Poets, dramatists, magicians, actors, sculptors, and artists of all kinds made the intellectual and aesthetic life of the empire brilliant. At first this seeming contradiction—a mercantile culture possessing great art works—puzzled me. Eventually, I realized that the great merchant families constituted the upper class and were in fact the only aristocracy permitted in the empire. And the aristocracy is essentially a leisure class, with both the spare time and the wealth to encourage the arts.

As soon as my injuries were healed I was bathed, carefully groomed, and herded into an enormous room with a large number of other slaves, both male and female, of every age and condition of health.

Seated on raised benches against the walls of this room, richly dressed men and women lolled. This was either a slave auction or an interrogation session, in which the talents and capabilities of newly acquired slaves would be ascertained. I soon discovered it was both at once.

In turn, each slave was brought before an examining committee which consisted of a physician, who swiftly estimated the slave's condition of bodily health, and interrogators who inquired pointedly into his or her background, training, experience, and education, if any. This data was then loudly announced by a fat, perspiring auctioneer to the assembled gentry, who discussed among themselves appropriate positions the slave might best fill. Sums of money were bandied back and forth, arguments occasionally broke out, and, on the whole, I found the occasion singularly boring. I must admit I had come to the slave block with my mind filled with preconceptions gained from observing imaginative reconstructions of such scenes in historical movies of the late Cecil B. DeMille. Mr. DeMille had an instinct for showmanship that must, occasionally, have shouted down his urge toward authenticity; for similar scenes in his films generally ran to brutal slave-handlers stripping beautiful girls before leering crowds of giggling perverts, or helpless slaves groveling under the lash of growling, heavy-handed guards much in need of a shave.

The scene, however, in which I myself now partook

was nothing like the cinematic version. The slaves were handled brusquely but imperonally, like cattle; I observed no brutalities nor indecencies. As for the audience, they were businessmen occupied with practical interests, not tittering perverts gathered for a show of sex and torture. They were a richly overdressed lot—for wealth in Narouk lends itself to ostentation—garbed in many-layered robes or gowns of gorgeous silks, in many colors, with peach, magenta, apple-green, and royal purple predominating. The robes were ornamented with gold fringe, tassels, gemmed belts and pectorals, dangling sashes, scraps of rare furs, and so on.

Both men and women wore an amazing amount of jewelry, rings sparkled on every finger, to say nothing of earrings, necklaces, brooches, pins, bracelets, gorgets, armlets, jeweled greaves, tiaras, and items of jewelry to which I could put no name. Some of the jewelry nearest me was truly spectacular: one woman, a proud matron of about fifty, turned to observe the slaves in my group and I suppressed a gasp at the immense gem she wore dangling from her forehead. It was the size of a child's fist, a rich purple jewel with an elusive flicker of scarlet flame in its heart—a jewel the Thanatorians call a *koromé* and for which I can think of no precise terrene equivalent.

What made this gem so unusual was its incredible rarity. Only a score such gems had ever been found, and this one, from its size, must have been worth a truly fabulous sum. You could have bought a kingdom with what this one Perushtarian woman wore on her hairless brow!

At length it was my turn to be interrogated. The questions were blunt and to the point. While the physician peered at my teeth, thumped my chest, slapped my biceps and thighs, scrutinized the condition of my now-healed lacerations, a team of questioners brusquely inquired as to my age, homeland, and areas of expertise. They had never heard of the United States of America, of course, but dutifully copied the term down, transliterated into the Thanatorian characters. They did not ask me why I had been aboard the *Jalathadar* seeming to have already formed the opinion that I was either a mercenary who had enlisted in the sky navy of Zanadar, or a slave pressed into service aboard the aerial galleon of the Sky Pirates.

Nor did I volunteer information to the contrary. It did not seem advisable for me to reveal my connections with Shondakor until I could gain a more accurate estimate of the political situation here. I was content, for the moment, to pass as merely another unimportant slave. And when asked my name, I replied that it was Darjan—a simple transposition of the syllables of the name the Thanatorians call me. This also seemed wise, and I resolved to conceal my true identity until I knew more of the situation in Narouk. It was not at all impossible that the Perushtarians were aware that one Jandar had been instrumental in wresting the city of Shondakor the Golden free of the detested yoke of the Black Legion. But they could know nothing of Darjan, as he had no history, having been invented on the spur of the moment.

"Now then, fellow, what training have you had?" demanded my chief interrogator.

"I am an excellent swordsman," I replied.

He fixed me with a sharp eye.

"As a slave, you will prefix all remarks to free men with the word 'master,'" he said curtly. I nodded acquiescence and rephrased the answer I had already given.

My questioner seemed unimpressed with further data on my abilities as a swordsman, which rather surprised me. I was, in fact, a master-swordsman, thanks to the advanced theoretical knowledge and practical experience of the art acquired at the Academy Lukor. Swordsmanship is a rare and difficult skill, which virtually every Thanatorian gentleman had to study.

However, as became apparent, it was not considered particularly desirable for a slave to know too much of the art of fence.

I was next interrogated as to my proficiency with the skills of reading, writing, and arithmetic. While I had in fact by now managed to acquire a working knowledge of the reading and writing of the Thanatorian charactery, my grasp was of the fundamentals only, and I was almost completely ignorant of the arithmetical arts as practiced on Callisto. The interrogators also quickly ascertained that I had neither knowledge or experience in sailing ships or their navigation, nor in farming, gardening, manufacture, pottery-making, or in any of the arts and crafts.

They exchanged a glance with each other and shrugged.

Then they passed a note along to the auctioneer on his elevated platform.

"Lot M-7709140-G13," he announced in his stentorian voice. "Name, Darjan. Homeland, the United States of America. Captured when fallen overboard from a Zanadarian vessel off the shores of the Corund Laj. Age, about thirty. Skills, swordsmanship; no others. Physical condition, quite fit, but probably not heavy enough in back and shoulders for galley oarsman or farmer."

High above, on the cushioned benches, my captor, Lord Cham, frowned busily over a bundle of documents, listening with half an ear. He now raised his eyes, looked me over, and shrugged.

"He has no needed skills. Add him to the Tribute."

There can be few circumstances in life more humiliating than to stand on the slave block and have one's various skills and qualifications summed up, only to learn that they total precisely nothing.

The situation would have been amusing had it not been so fraught with unknown danger. That these practical, hardheaded businessmen of Perushtar should reject as unfit for any known occupation a man of my extraordinary breadth of experience upon two planets was a blow to my ego, which is as healthy as that of any man. That I, who had ventured alone into the cloud-girt city of Zanadar, to rescue from the very stronghold of Prince Thuton the beautiful princess of Shondakor—I, who had braved a thousand perils, who had penetrated under disguise the secret councils of the Black Legion, who had battled and adventured my way across half a planet ere now, and who had won the love of the Ku Thad nation, the admiration of a loyal band of trusted comrades, and the heart of the most beautiful woman in two worlds—should be ranked among the human rejects and discards, set aside by the oligarchs of Narouk as of no worth and value, was a devastating injury to my self-esteem.

Nevertheless, while I gaped in astonishment over my sentence, guards hustled me from the room to an adjoining pen wherein were assembled a motley crew of the ill, the crippled, the witless, the deformed, the uncooperative, and the vicious. To this unappetizing company my person was added. My neck chain was secured to a link in the line. Then the guards left the chamber and I squatted helpless and seething with rage beside my fellow rejects.

To my left was a rheumy-eyed, bony-shanked old gaffer devoid of teeth, who wheezed and rattled as if every moment might he his last in this mortal sphere.

To my right was chained a witless, drooling incompetent, whose glazed, indifferent eyes and slack jaw denoted the state of a mindless vegetable.

And between these two prizes was chained Jandar of Callisto, hero of a thousand battles, and the greatest swordsman of two worlds.

Later on, once the sting of rejection wore off, I might well find the entire situation hilarious. At the moment, however, I boiled with resentment and vowed vengeance on the careless oligarchs of Narouk, who could not see a first-class fighting man when he stood before them.

Ere long my temper cooled somewhat and permitted apprehension to enter where anger had reigned.

I was assigned to the Tribute, to the nameless legion of doomed and desperate men whose fate was an enigma, and this was the peculiar and dreaded disposition of unwanted slaves whereof I had first heard but tantalizingly little, that time, early during my period of slavery, when I had by chance overheard the old slave Kenelon and the woman Imarra in conversation.

I recalled, with an inward shudder I give my reader leave to picture for himself, how Kenelon and Imarra had discussed the mysterious doom of those given over to the Tribute. And now I had good and sound reason to curse my caution. For, having acquired a morsel of information not intended for my ears, and which I deemed might be of value to me in the days ahead, I had refrained from asking Kenelon about the Tribute when the chance had been offered me.

Of course, I had then no way of knowing how

swiftly my doom would be upon me. But, still, I now cursed myself for not simply asking him what it was all about when I had had the opportunity.

Toward what enigmatic destiny was I now impelled?

Tribute to whom—to *what*?

To the gore-drenched altars of some barbaric god? Or the torments of some savage race, whose invasion was delayed by offering of human tribute?

What *was* it that I was to be offered in tribute to?

No man knew. But I would soon be finding out— and by the hard way.

Together with the rest of this shambling horde of the crippled, the deformed, the idiotic, and the unfit, I was herded from the villa to an outdoor slave-pen on the edge of the city where we spent a miserable night huddled under cold and sleety skies, watched by a heavy guard of alert warriors.

And with morning we were on our way out of the city of Narouk, bound for an unknown destination and a mysterious doom.

Book III

THE FROZEN LAND

Chapter 7

OUT OF CONTROL!

And now I have come to that point in my narrative where I must describe incidents to which I was not a witness—adventures in which I did not personally partake.

At the time of their occurrence, I was completely ignorant of these events, and it was only long after their conclusion that I learned of them.

It was Koja of the Yathoon Horde who was the first to notice that I was no longer aboard the *Jalathadar*.

The giant arthopode gradually became aware of my absence. The aerial contrivance, in which we had intended to voyage to the City in the Clouds, had risen from the surface of the Corund Laj into the brilliant daylight. The supplies of fresh drinking water now fully replenished, the sky ship ascended rapidly to the three-thousand-foot level and proceeded due west in the direction of the White Mountains.

The shores of the great inland sea rapidly receded in the wake of the flying galleon. The domes and tower of Narouk vanished on the horizon; Ganatol, too, sped beneath the keel of the sky machine. Soon the *Jalathadar* would be over the hill country, and ere many hours had passed, it would be flying over the great mountain range itself, bound for the mountaintop citadel of the infamous Sky Pirates.

At first, Koja suspected nothing. The huge insect-man merely noticed that I was no longer to be seen on the midship deck. Some time before, the arthopode had noticed me lounging by the rail; now that he looked again, I was no longer there. Instead, it was the Zanadarian captive, Ulthar, who leaned idly against the carven balustrade.

Koja came stalking up to where the former captain of the *Jalathadar* stood.

"Has Jandar gone below or up to the control cupola?" the faithful Yathoon Warrior inquired in his solemn, uninflected voice.

Ulthar darted an alert, wary glance at the chitin-clad giant. Then his eyes fell away with seeming indifference.

"I have not seen him, *kapok*," Ulthar replied.

Koja's chitinous casque of a face was devoid of expression, and his enormous compound eyes reflected no expression as he observed the Zanadarian captive, who fidgeted nervously under his solemn scrutiny.

"But he was here at the rail just a few moments before we ascended," Koja said patiently. "I was aloft, and I remember seeing you stroll over to where he stood, leaning against the rail. Surely, you must have noticed in which direction he went when he quit your company...."

"I said I saw him not! An end to your questions, *kapok!*" Ulthar snapped, abruptly.

The huge eyes surveyed the nervous Sky Pirate imperturbably. "*Kapok*" is a derogatory term sometimes used against the Yathoon insect-men as an insult. It may be translated as "bug." Koja did not enjoy hearing that term applied to him, but, not being human, his reactions were not those of an ordinary warrior. Indeed, the arthopodes of Thanator do not experience the full range of human emotions, and are popularly thought to have no emotions at all, since their endocrine system is markedly different from that of the other races of the Jungle Moon. This, however, is a fallacy. I had taught Koja the meaning of friendship, and he had found his own way to love, for I believe the stalking, ungainly monstrosity loved me with an unswerving devotion and loyalty rare even in men.

He did not, however, react to the insult, but stood, blinking emotionlessly down at the tense, fidgeting Zanadarian. Perhaps his cool intelligence was pondering the motive behind the other's nervousness and short temper, or perhaps he was slowly rephrasing the question in his mind. At any rate, with a snarled expletive, the Zanadarian prisoner abruptly turned from the rail and strode rapidly away.

Koja stared after him, pondering the strangeness of his mood and actions. Then he ascended to the control cupola to see if I had gone there, but of course he found me not—for at that moment I was floundering in the beach shallows, exhaustedly struggling to drag myself up onto the shoreline.

Valkar was duty officer at the time, it being his shift. The handsome Ku Thad prince greeted the solemn-faced insect-man in a friendly fashion and replied that he had not seen me in some time.

"Jandar is not on duty at present, and may be taking his leisure in his cabin. Why don't you look there?"

Koja thanked him and turned away. But I was not in my cabin, nor in the galley, nor down in the store chambers, nor in the wheel deck, nor in the poop. I did not seem to be anywhere aboard the *Jalathadar!*

This, the Yathoon warrior found puzzling in the extreme. But where a human being might have taken alarm at this point, the cool, disciplined mind of the stalking arthopode merely registered the accumulated data and continued patiently in his methodical search, until, sometime later, he had ascertained that I was simply not on board at all.

Having made certain of my absence, however, Koja wasted no time in bringing the matter to the attention of his comrades.

Lukor's cabin adjoined my own, Koja entered, to find the gallant, silver-haired little swordmaster reclining comfortably on his bunk, sharing his attention equally between a black bottle of well-aged brandy and a volume of salacious anecdotes called *The Thousand Diversions of Pellasitir the Inventive*. The amiable Ganatolian waved a greeting as the solemn-faced insectoid entered his quarters.

"Hoy, friend Koja! You find me at my leisure, improving my mind with a brief but informative excursions into the less reputable byways of literature and restoring my depleted energies with an excellent bottle of *quarra*, of a vintage vastly overrated by injudicious connoisseurs, but not without a robust bouquet to recommend it. There is nothing like a well-aged *quarra* . . . how does the poet put it? 'The golden nectar of a vanished summer slumbers in the good wine's honied heart'—is something wrong?"

"Jandar is not on board," said Koja in flat, emotionless tones, going right to the point as was his usual way. The peppery little Ganatolian, who had been refreshing himself with another swig from the black bottle, as if to test the wisdom of the poet whom he had just quoted, choked on the fiery beverage.

"*Ak-kaff! Umph!* My jointed friend, whatever are you talking about? Of course our brave and yellow-headed captain is aboard—wherever else could he be, may I ask, and us three thousand feet above the ground?"

"Lukor, he is nowhere on the ship. I have searched the vessel from stem to stern, and he is not to be found. Something untoward has occurred. . . ."

Lukor tossed his book aside with a muttered curse, corked the brandy bottle, tenderly deposited it beneath his pillow, and sat up on the edge of the bunk, sobering at Koja's ominous words.

"You suspect foul play, is that it?"

Koja flexed his brow-antennae in the Yathoon equivalent of a human shrug of the shoulders.

"I saw him at the rail while we were taking on fresh supplies of water. Now he is nowhere aboard the galleon. I asked the Zanadarian, Ulthar, which way Jandar had gone, but he professed ignorance on the matter. However, he could hardly have avoided seeing our friend leave, since he was rather near him at the time. It is a puzzle, Lukor."

Lukor massaged his brow and tugged viciously at his long, carefully tended mustachios.

"Ulthar, is it? I would not trust that Zanadarian any further than I could throw him . . . and I would be happy to attempt throwing him, if the deck rail was near enough! I warned Jandar he was making a mistake by permitting that treacherous, sly, cunning rascal of a Sky Pirate to voyage with us—but it is always our noble captain's way to expect the best of others, rather than anticipating the worst from them. Well, if Ulthar has had a hand in this, we shall not find it difficult to pry his tongue loose—I know a little trick with a heated dagger-blade set between the bare toes that will encourage the most close-mouthed man on Thanator to pour forth his autobiography in less time than it takes to heat the blade. But—caution, now— have you thoroughly searched the ship? Our friend may well be gossiping with one of the officers in their several cabins or down in the hold with the men, swapping a bottle and telling tall tales of derring-do...."

Koja described the itinerary of his search. By the time he had completed his account, the excitable little Ganatolian master-swordsman was alarmed.

"Where is Prince Valkar? In the control cupola, you say? Come, friend Koja, we must bring this to the attention of the ship's company at once, before we have traveled farther. Jandar may well have fallen overboard."

"Or been pushed," said Koja expressionlessly.

Ere long the alarm was given, and anxious men combed every cubicle and closet of the *Jalathadar* without finding any token of my whereabouts. Summoned before a worried Valkar, our captive Sky Pirate stubbornly maintained that he knew nothing of my whereabouts—which was, I suppose, true enough, for Ulthar could not have known that by this time I had been taken prisoner by the lord Cham of Narouk, and he doubtless assumed or at least hoped that I had drowned beneath the blue waves of the Corund Laj, weighed down by my boots, sword, cloak, and other encumbrances.

No threats of stern measures could dislodge the truth from the smooth-tongued Zanadarian, who eloquently argued his complete ignorance in the matter and his innocence of any wrongdoing.

"Give me a few moments alone with this sky rascal, a dagger blade and a pot of coals from the galley, and I will pry the truth from him!" Lukor demanded. But Valkar reluctantly forbade any such questioning by force.

"We cannot do that, Lukor. We have Captain Ulthar's word of his innocence, and nothing against him but idle suspicion. Why, even Koja cannot offer us eyewitness proof of wrongdoing! It is entirely possible that Jandar fell overboard, taken off-balance when the *Jalathadar* lifted, or borne away by a strong gust of wind sometime later on. But to subject a helpless captive, who has given us his parole and his oath of honor not to interfere with the functioning of the ship, would be an act of criminal barbarism. We are, after all, civilized men."

" 'Civilized men,' are we?" Lukor spat, as if the very phrase left a bad taste in his mouth. "Well, maybe so, and maybe a wee touch of uncivilized behavior, would wring the truth from this smooth-tongued assassin," he fumed.

But Valkar would not listen to such words. He did, however, everything that could be done under such mysterious circumstances. The aerial galleon swung about and retraced the leagues she had traveled, regaining again her former position above the bright waves of the Greater Sea. Anxious eyes combed the waters for any sign of me, and armed parties prowled the nearer shores, but by then I imagine the waves in their ceaseless advance and retreat had smoothed away the footprints I had made when I had emerged from the sea, for my friends found nothing to suggest I had come ashore.

For many hours the gigantic flying machine hovered above land and sea, searching for the lost adventurer. Far into the night the sky ship floated above the grassy hills, alert for the slightest token of my presence. But, of course, I was not to be found, for by that time I was sound asleep on my rude pallet in the slave pens of Narouk.

Fuming at the frustration imposed by inactivity, the peppery little swordmaster was all for storming the walls and gates of Narouk—or, rather, he urged Valkar to descend upon the central market square of the city, demanding that I be turned over to the ship, if indeed I was being held captive by the Perushtarians. Valkar himself was rather given to this idea, for indeed it seemed logical that if I had somehow gone overboard while the sky galleon was lifting from the waters of the Corund Laj, I could well have been taken captive by a party of Perushtarian warriors.

But the responsibility of sole command had now devolved upon the strong shoulders of the Shondakorian prince, and he could not yield to the temptation. For the prime purpose of our voyage into peril was and must remain the setting free of Princess Darloona from her captivity among the Sky Pirates. And to imperil the entire quest on a hare-brained scheme was to jeopardize her safety, which was—and remained—of paramount concern.

Until the princess of Shondakor was safe among her friends, any man aboard the *Jalathadar*—even myself—must be considered expendable. And for one lone ship to attack a full-sized city was to risk the damage or destruction of the ship—and the doom of Darloona, warrior princess of the Ku Thad.

Valkar wrestled mightily with his decision. He and I were old comrades and many was the time we had fought side by side or back to back, holding death away at swords' length. For him to desert me now in the hour of my greatest peril was the most horrendous decision he had ever been forced to make, but in the lonely eminence of his captaincy, he had to make that decision, although no other man can ever know the immense agony he endured in reaching his eventual choice of action.

Against the darkness of the night sky, where the

great moons of Jupiter spread their multicolored rays across the silent landscape, the *Jalathadar* rose on silent wings, the last footsore and bone-weary search party having been taken aboard.

Then she turned her prow towards distant Zanadar and sailed off into the night, leaving me a doomed and helpless captive in the hands of the Perushtarians.

Sometime before dawn Valkar was rudely roused from his exhausted slumbers. He propped himself up on one elbow and peered blearily into the light of a swaying lamp held by Lukor.

"What . . . what is it? What's wrong, Lukor?"

" 'What is it?' indeed, my fine prince!" chortled the spry old Ganatolian with a sort of fierce, grim enjoyment. "Perhaps, one of these days, when enough disasters have overtaken us, the excellent Lord Valkar will begin to pay some attention to the timely warnings of a garrulous old swordsman! *Hah!*"

Valkar blinked at him, understanding none of this. Behind the little Ganatolian loomed the silent Koja, lamplight striking highlights on the glistening, expressionless mask of his chitinous face, solemn eyes glittering.

"What are you talking about? What's happened now?" demanded Valkar.

Lukor snorted. "Oh, nothing—nothing at all! It's just that the trustworthy Zanadarian, who gave you his word of honor not to violate his parole or to do aught to interfere with the operation of the vessel—which word of honor you chose over my poor arguments—has cut the wing lines and wrecked the steering controls."

"*What?*" Valkar demanded incredulously. His gaze flew past Lukor to meet Koja's emotionless eyes.

"It is true, Valkar," the arthopode intoned somberly. "The vessel can no longer be steered, and is plunging before a powerful tailwind, completely out of control."

Valkar ground out a bitter curse between clenched teeth, swung his legs over the edge of the bunk, and came to his feet, snatching on the garments he had discarded at retiring.

"How . . . how did this happen?"

Lukor's face was screwed into a smug expression that wavered between a scowl and a smile.

"Why, through treachery—treason—cunning lies!" he barked. " 'Pray, honorable Valkar, let me take this sneaking scum aside and question him a bit with a slight application of heated steel' 'Oh, no,' quoth you, 'we cannot do that to so fine and trustworthy a gentleman as the noble Ulthar! Be silent, you silly old Ganatolian! 'Twould be rude—crude—criminous! Step aside, you white-bearded old barbarian, and permit the gently born Ulthar to go about his business—' "

"Oh, *do* be quiet, Lukor!" cried the exasperated Valkar. "What is our current situation? Are we losing altitude, or what? What's our position—and have you apprehended Ulthar, or is he still on the loose?"

Koja's face was devoid of expression and his voice was an emotionless monotone as he replied.

"That is another mystery, Valkar. For, having accomplished his dirty work, the Zanadarian traitor has vanished completely. We have searched the ship from stem to stern, and he is nowhere on board. *He has vanished, just like Jandar. . . .*"

Chapter 8

THE MYSTERIOUS NORTH

Valkar scrambled into his clothes and ascended swiftly into the control cupola, where he was quickly
brought abreast of their situation.

Duty officer for that watch of the night had been a
young noble called Tomar. An impressionable, easily
influenced youth, the boy had generally taken everyone at his word (a trait that Lukor had earlier as-
cribed to me, as well). Some of the men had noticed
that our captive had exchanged friendly words with
the impressionable youth on several occasions, but no
one had thought much of it. And quite frequently,
complaining he was unable to sleep, Ulthar had
shared the lonely night-watch with the young Shondakorian noble.

Ulthar was forbidden the control cupola, but had
taken his station in one of the observation belvederes
nearby and, while scrupulously avoiding any inter-
ference with Tomar's watch, had from time to time
given him tips on navigation and some slight advice
on trimming the wheel. No one had thought much of
this, either.

On this particular night, however, again claiming
he was unable to sleep, Ulthar had casually leaned
against the balustrade of the observation belvedere,
and had, in his friendly, unobtrusive way, quietly en-

gaged the boy in desultory conversation during this loneliest of watches.

A strong wind had sprung up during the night, buffeting the *Jalathadar* to starboard and requiring constant attention to the wheel to avoid being driven off course by imperceptible degrees. It was not an emergency, but it demanded the duty officer's fullest attention. Chatting casually, Ulthar had given the boy a few words of advice on holding the ship steady and a bit later had advised him that the craft might easily rise again above the buffeting winds by ascending a few hundred more feet. The trusting young officer had complied with these bits of advice, lifting the ship to a higher level, and at that altitude the vessel had encountered a powerful tailwind blowing due north.

Ulthar now advised the boy to have the rudder trimmed to offset this new influence on the course, and before the youth could rouse his messenger, who slumbered soundly in the cupola against call, the smooth-tongued Zanadarian volunteered to go back and pass the order along. There was simply no reason why Tomar should have suspected the wily Sky Pirate of treachery, so he accepted the other's offer and passed down to him the code flag which denoted an official steering command, and which all messengers bore under such circumstances.

But instead of going aft to the rudder station, Ulthar muffled himself in his hooded cloak, which he had donned against the cold winds of this height, and, wordlessly showing the official code flag, had gone down to the wheel decks, unattended except by a skeleton crew at this hour. There, unrecognized in the uncertain light, his few gruff commands given in a disguised voice, Ulthar bade the crewmen go on deck to help unlimber the shroud lines. And once the deck was cleared, he opened a wall cabinet, where a fire ax was kept against emergencies, and proceeded to sever one by one the great cables that carried motive power from the wheels to the hinged wing-sections. He had crippled one entire wing and was busily chopping away the cables that controlled the other, when a curious member of the wheel crew descended to question the order, which no one on deck knew anything about.

Ulthar had cut the man down with one blow of the great ax, but others were crowding down the gangway by then, so, leaving the starboard wing only partially damaged, the traitorous Sky Pirate had turned and fled.

And was nowhere to be found, although the crippled ship had been thoroughly searched.

He had simply vanished into thin air!

Tomar had, it was soon discovered, ascended into a very dangerous altitude, higher than any at which we had yet sailed the *Jalathadar*.

A seasoned and veteran sailor of the skies of Thanator, Ulthar had surely known this, known that at the three-thousand-foot level, subtle but powerful up-drafts from the winding canyons of the mountainous country below can gradually and imperceptibly lift the keel of a Zanadarian ornithopter many hundreds of feet over the hours of darkness. Doubtless his desultory conversation, combined with the efforts required to hold the galleon steady on her course against the buffeting pressure of the cross-winds, had so occupied the young officer's mind that he had not noticed the sky ship was ascending ever higher at a steady but unobtrusive pace.

Then, timing his action to a nicety, remembering

those coded charts of the wind belts of Thanator we had labored fruitlessly without deciphering, Ulthar had at exactly the proper time casually advised the boy officer to ascend a few hundred feet to escape the buffeting winds—which brought the *Jalathadar*, unbeknownst to any but the cunning Ulthar himself, into a powerful south-to-north windstream, which, at the vessel's four-thousand-foot level, stood at gale force.

As these grim facts and deductions sank in, Valkar ground his teeth. The calamity was all but disastrous, and while the ship was not completely crippled, she was at least helpless to evade the gale winds which blew her on and on into the unknown north of the world.

With one wing out of action and the other only partially useful, the rudder alone was not sufficient to alter the course of the *Jalathadar*.

A helpless prisoner of the winds, she flew steadily across the mountain country, drawing farther and farther from her goal. Ahead of her lay leagues of bleak and barren arctic tundra, where no man dwelt and no cities existed.

Ahead lay the glittering ice fields of the polar cap and a horrible death at the ultimate north of the world.

And there was nothing they could do about it.

Dawn broke, flushing the skies of the Jungle Moon with pallid gold.

Driven before the merciless fury of the gale wind, the giant ornithopter flew steadily on into the unknown regions of the mysterious north.

In the captain's cabin, Valkar and the other senior officers pored wearily over the coded charts, striving to figure out a solution to their dilemma.

Unable to assist in the solution of their navigational problems, Lukor and Koja prowled the great ship restlessly, hoping against hope itself that they would somehow stumble upon the hiding place of the traitor, Ulthar.

With them, white-faced, with haunted eyes, went the boy Tomar. Tortured by feelings of guilt for his unconscious complicity in the cunning plot of the treacherous Zanadarian, the young noble suffered acutely. His sufferings were somehow all the more unendurable in that none of his shipmates had as yet uttered the slightest word of condemnation against him. The boy would have felt better, oddly enough, had they hurled accusations at his head, cursing him for a vapid fool.

Instead, they had said nothing at all. Valkar had slapped him on the shoulder in silent sympathy, tousled his hair affectionately, and had muttered a few comforting words to the effect that he should not blame himself for this calamity. Of course, the boy did indeed blame himself—and curse himself for an easily swayed idiot—and would cheerfully have laid down his life, could self-sacrifice have alleviated his responsibility for the disaster in any degree.

Bluff, garrulous, kind-hearted old Lukor, sensing the silent boy's inward torments, loudly tried to josh him out of his black mood.

"Tush, lad, 'tis not your fault—yonder slick-tongued rapscalion could charm the fish out of the seas with his words! Look how he bemused Prince Valkar with his protestations of innocence, when not a man of the crew but had the slightest doubt that our tall Koja here was correct in his suspicions and that the lying villain tipped poor Jandar over the side when we were taking on water. You mustn't blame yourself, m'boy."

The young officer shook his head stubbornly, without a word, but his bright, tearless eyes were eloquent. Even Koja was disturbed by the lad's eloquent suffering. The gaunt, chitin-clad, ungainly arthopode—so invulnerable to human emotions—touched the boy's shoulder with an awkward, tentative caress.

"You must listen to Lukor, now. He speaks the truth, you know. No one blames you in the slightest, young Tomar, and it is thus irrational for you to blame yourself."

"I can't help it, Lord Koja—Master Lukor—I should have known better than to trust him. But . . . he was so casual and offhand about it all, and we had spoken several times before. I knew he was an enemy and not to be trusted, but—but—I guess I felt sorry for him, alone among strangers, with no one to give him a kind word. So I just fell into the habit of smiling, and saying hello, and sort of passing the time of day, a little. . . ."

"Ah, the cunning rascal, to play upon the kindly feelings of a well-meaning boy," Lukor snarled.

They paused by the deck rail, viewing the barren land ahead, bathed in the brilliant morning light.

"'Tis a strange land into which we venture, comrades," said Lukor. "I, for one, know naught of the northlands. What of yourself, friend Koja?"

The towering insectoid stared solemnly out across the bleak tundra toward the glittering ice ramparts on the distant horizon.

"My people inhabit the southernmost portion of the globe, as you know, Lukor, and upon the endless grasslands of the Great Plains of Haratha was I hatched and raised to adulthood. Never do the war parties of my clan venture north of the Grand Kumala, and in all my days I have never journeyed beyond the ramparts of the White Mountains. But my people have vague traditions of the north of the world, the Frozen Land, as we call it. There is naught within those traditions that is the least wholesome."

Lukor surveyed the northern horizon bemusedly.

"Well, I come from Ganatol, as you know, but we Ganatolians know a bit of the country north of the mountains and, like your own people of the Yathoon Horde, we have heard naught that is wholesome of the Frozen Land. However, ere long we shall discover the truth behind these unsavory myths, eh, comrades?"

Koja's gaze was fathomless, his jeweled black eyes inscrutable.

"I begin to understand the actions of the villain Ulthar," he said in his cold monotone. "The man thrust Jandar overboard, hoping we would waste time searching for him and perhaps do something foolish, like getting embroiled in a raid against the Perushtarian city of Narouk, to the possible detriment of our quest to Zanadar. But when that ploy proved fruitless, and we persisted in our intention to sail against the City in the Clouds, even without Jandar at our side, he must have staked all on a desperate gamble to cripple the ship so that it would be caught helpless in the gale winds of the four-thousand-foot level and be carried into the Frozen Land, there to crash among the ice mountains which legends hint may be found at the pole of the world. A clever and resourceful man, this Ulthar—a pity that he is against us and not with us. . . ."

The boy Tomar spoke up now; the warm, friendly words of Lukor and Koja seemed to have broken through his preoccupation with his fancied guilt. "I wonder where he is hiding. Do you suppose there is some sort of a secret compartment on the ship, somewhere?"

Koja manipulated his antenna in the Yathoon version of a shrug.

"Perhaps so," his grating voice said tonelessly. "Or perhaps, his mission accomplished, he threw himself overboard to avoid his certain punishment at the hands of Prince Valkar. Such fanaticism is not uncommon among humans, I believe. We of the Yathoon Horde are often accused of fatalism, but it has been my experience that human beings are themselves far from invulnerable against the desire for self-immolation."

"Well, if he *is* hiding somewhere aboard the ship, oughtn't we to be on the lookout for him?" Tomar suggested. "Surely, he's bound to get hungry, and will have to come out of hiding or starve to death. We might be able to grab him then, when he does come out!"

Lukor stroked his neatly trimmed white beard judiciously.

"The boy has a point there, Koja," he mused. "But *I* am thinking that if Ulthar is indeed hidden somewhere aboard the ship, he will be thinking more about that undamaged rudder and starboard wing than he will about his empty stomach. It would not be at all unlike the sneaking rascal to come creeping out of his secret hidey-hole, when all are asleep, to disable the last maneuverable portions of the ship. Best we advise Valkar to mount watch tonight, lest any such 'accidents' occur; we are in enough trouble right now, as things already stand."

"He doesn't even have to do that," Tomar spoke up again. "Do you know what would be the worst possible thing Ulthar could do against us? If he still has that fire ax with him, he could chop a hole right through the double-hull and let all of the gas out . . . then we'd crash and be shattered against the ground.

And that would really be the end of everything. . . ."

"Hmm," muttered Lukor, stroking his beard thoughtfully. "The lad has something there, Koja. Best we bring these notions to the attention of Prince Valkar without delay!"

The three turned and left the deck rail in search of the captain.

All that day the *Jalathadar* hurtled on into the mysterious north. It grew steadily colder; ice began to form on the rigging and, ere nightfall, the rigid wings were sheathed in sparkling crystal.

They were over the great ice fields of the polar cap now; some of them wondered if the winds could carry them on across the ultimate pole and into the other hemisphere of Thanator, a region of utter mystery, or whether the winds would lose their force and dwindle in intensity once they were near the pole itself.

No one really knew.

But already new dangers were presenting themselves, for as the wing surfaces and decks became sheathed in sparkling ice, the deposits added to the weight of the vessel, and she began to sink lower and lower.

With darkness, the land below became obscured, save for the feeble luminance provided by the slowly rising moons. Below them lay a glittering sea of ice, like a vast desert of molten glass. But to the north, blotting out the faint glimmer of the all-but-invisible stars, rose sharp peaks; whether these were mountains of solid ice, as legends whispered, or were merely mountains of rock, could not be ascertained. Neither did it really matter; what did matter was the *height* of those mountains.

Were they high enough to endanger the lumbering

Jalathadar, rapidly sinking under the cumulative weight of her ice?

Would they rush on until they crashed full into the peak of one of those mountains, looming up before them out of the darkness—a mountain they could not avoid, due to the damage Ulthar had wrought to their steering apparatus?

In the face of this all-too-possible danger, Valkar had no patience with idle theories about skulking saboteurs concealed in secret compartments that might or might not be hidden within the structure of the giant ornithopter. He did, however, take the precaution of stationing guards over the undamaged wing, control cupola, and rudder.

Sinking lower and lower with every hour, her decks sheathed with solid ice, the galleon of the skies began to lose speed as she descended below the four-thousand-foot level. But black night had closed down around her by now, and even the great and many-colored moons of Thanator were hidden behind thick banks of blowing fog, filled with driving sleet.

There was little sleep for any of the men that night, aboard the galleon of the skies, which we had most aptly named the *Desperate Venture.*

One of the senior officers, sturdy old Haakon it was, had proposed a risky plan to bring the *Jalathadar* to a halt so that her wing cables could be rewoven.

It was his plan to use what little maneuverability they had to bring the flying ship near the peaks of the mountains, and to fire our catapult at the nearest of the peaks.

Earlier in this narrative I have already discussed the giant steel arrows the smiths of Shondakor the Golden had prepared for this "secret weapon" of mine. Well, Haakon suggested they secure a strong line about the

shaft of one or several of these arrows, and fire them
into the ice-clad peaks, an act that might—just might
—bring the *Jalathadar* to a halt, similar to using an
anchor to secure a sea-going ship against the actions
of the tides.

The scheme was fraught with perils, of course.

The lines might not hold, in which case they would
lose their arrows, and the catapult would be rendered
useless.

Conversely, the lines might hold, but the sudden
halting of the ship in midflight might batter her to
wreckage against the mountain peaks, or the winds
might tear her apart.

It was a desperate plan, but it might well succeed,
and the officers agreed it was worth a try. Anything
was better than flying blind through the unmapped
mountains of the pole and either smashing the ship to
atoms by collision in the dark with one such peak or
being blown over the pole to be lost amid the unknown dangers of the mysterious hemisphere beyond.

So Valkar roused all the ship's company, stationing
men along the deck rails, in the masthead observa-
tion-points and along the various ports, with lamps
and torches to provide what little illumination they
could, while the slowing winds blew the ice-sheathed
ship among the frozen peaks of the pole, and a band
of trained gunnery officers stood ready to fire the catapult.

One member of the crew, however, had not been
able to get out of his mind the possibility that Ulthar
was still hidden somewhere on the ship.

It was young Tomar.

The boy still felt keenly his guilt in unconsciously
giving the treacherous Zanadarian his chance to disable the flying galleon of the skies.

So while the rest of the ship's company were busied on deck with the dangerous scheme to harpoon a mountain peak and bring the *Jalathadar* to a halt, young Tomar went into the untenanted captain's cabin to search through the ship's papers, hunting for a chart or blueprint of the galleon itself.

The rest of us had long since given over the study of the ship's papers, for their coded notation had resisted our every effort to decipher them. The geographical charts, the ship's log, the signal book, the packets of standing orders—all these were deemed useless to us, unless we could solve the mystery of the Zanadarian code.

But the boy Tomar was not concerned with the solution of the code system. Before long he found a tightly rolled parchment scroll which served as a sort of blueprint of the ship's design, and was busily examining it by the light of a stealthy candle.

Cabin by cabin, chamber by chamber, closet by closet, the youth was studying the chart, comparing his knowledge of every hallway and compartment with the plan inked on the parchment scroll.

Somewhere in this chart he hoped to find a discrepancy.

One of the compartments inked here might very well not match with those familiar to his memory.

And that compartment, when he located it, would be the secret hiding place.

And in that compartment he would find Ulthar.

Chapter 9

ULTHAR'S LAIR

It was a weird, fantastic scene: the dark, windswept sky, the ice plateau under the many-colored glory of the huge moons of Jupiter, the flying ship wallowing sluggishly against the wind, sheathed in glittering ice, hurtling toward the sharp and jagged pinnacles of the ice mountains dead ahead.

One peak swept up before the swaying ornithopter. The light of the many moons flashed and sparkled from its crest of splintered pinnacles, rose, argent, deep yellow, gray-blue. It swung out of the darkness, loomed up before the prow, and the hurtling *Jalathadar* sped directly for it.

The ice mountain grew swollen and enormous. It blocked half the sky dead ahead. Any second the ship would ram straight into the glittering barrier, the figurehead would splinter, the prow crack, the hull shatter, precious levitating gas hissing like a thousand angry serpents as it leaked from burst hull-seams.

But Valkar had calculated to the last notch. Leaning crazily from the swaying cupola, dark red hair streaming behind him in the shrieking wind, he hoarsely bawled the order at the last possible instant of time.

Burly shoulders slammed into the great wheels. Guy stays creaked, timbers groaned, taut lines, rigid within their frozen envelope, thrummed like deep-throated harps in the roar of the gale. The great vans lifted, took another pitch, while desperate men thrust the vast rudder over with every atom of strength they could drain from knotted sinews. Backs straining, faces black with effort, they hurled their bodies against the control rods, battling to turn the rudder against the bellowing gale.

Lurching drunkenly, the *Jalathadar* staggered, swung about, swerved in the nick of time to swing safely past the ice peak. So narrow was her escape that the starboard wingtip scraped ice from the utmost pinnacle as she swung about.

And in that fraction of a second, old Lukor, in charge of the catapult crew in my absence, cut the thong. Like a gigantic bow wielded by a titan, the timbers of the catapult thundered home, launching the massive arrow of steel into the seething gale. The keen tip crunched deep in solid ice; hooked barbs held fast against the lurch of the mighty ship.

The *Jalathadar* wobbled, jolted to a dead stop, and swung back against the sheer wall of ice.

The impact was staggering. Men, stationed along the rails, went rolling into the scuppers like ten pins. Taut rigging, stretched beyond endurance, snapped. One mast splintered, broke clean, and the whistling winds ripped it away, crow's nest and all. The lone watchman stationed therein was whipped away, a quick glimpse of flailing limbs, a broken, despairing cry—and he was gone.

The ship came crunching up against the mountain peak. The deck rail crumpled under the impact. One forward-hull belvedere was shorn away. But, luckily, the damage was slight—slighter than anyone could have guessed. Gallant men hurled lassos about pinnacles. Steel grapnels crunched and squealed on slick ice. Soon many lines held the flying galleon fast against the peak of the mountain.

And Valkar began to breathe again.

The boy Tomar had found that for which he sought. The plans he had discovered among the ship's papers showed a small cubicle off B-deck, tucked away behind the captain's salon and the storage rooms that lay next to the double hull. The youth was certain that, in all his wanderings about the flying ship, he had never observed that cubicle. It *must* be the place whereat Ulthar lay hidden.

Taking up a lantern and his rapier, the young lieutenant determined to find out the truth for himself.

Down the swaying ladder he went, trying to ignore the pitch and toss as the ship rolled sluggishly to the beating gale. Shielding the lamp against accident, he felt his way down the swinging ladder until he reached the hallway, and thence along the narrow corridor, past the doors that led to the grand salon where the captain was wont to feast with his senior officers.

Twice he retraced the way, each time finding no entrance to any such cubicle. His eyes gleamed; he was certain he was right. But, if the cubicle could not be entered from the hall, it must have some sort of secret entrance through the grand salon itself. Greatly daring, the boy crept into the salon, his lamp muffled now under his cloak.

The walls were covered with bookshelves and brackets, between ribbed stanchions.

Somewhere here there must be a secret door.

But *where?*

He ran his fingers along the bottom edges of the

shelves, groping and testing for a secret catch, but he found nothing. He peered at the paneling, but the light of the many moons that shone in a fitful glare through the great bank of windows that overlooked the captain's balcony revealed nothing.

Then his questing fingers caught and dislodged a heavy navigational instrument of polished brass. It fell to the floor with a crash and rolled the length of the room with a frightful clatter, as the floor swayed to the pitch and roll of the ship. The boy held his breath, but nothing stirred.

He turned away then, to begin a careful examination of the entire wall, starting with the far corner. As he strode off, one panel slid aside, revealing a small opening. Keen black eyes glared through that hole, watching him as he went. Then unseen fingers touched a secret spring and a narrow section of wall slid aside with a faint hiss whose sound was lost in the bellowing of the gale.

And Tomar suspected nothing until suddenly, from behind, a strong arm locked about his throat and he stared up into the grim smiling features of Ulthar.

Choked into unconsciousness, the boy slid limply to the floor. Ulthar knelt swiftly, stripped him of dagger and sword, and removed the guttering oil-lamp from its precarious place, wrapped in Tomar's cloak. With a malicious chuckle, the Sky Pirate ensconced the lamp in a nearby wall-bracket. It would never do, he smiled to himself, to permit the lamp to fall and perhaps break, thus turning the *Jalathadar* into a raging inferno.

Having disarmed the unconscious youth, he stepped swiftly across the salon to the door, listened intently, peered out, taking great care that he should not be seen. Then, satisfied that the youth had come alone, he crossed the room to where Tomar sprawled and stood looking down at him thoughtfully.

Probably the best and safest thing to do would be to slit the lad's throat right now and heave him out the windows. That way no one would be able to trace him to Ulthar's secret hiding place—but, stay! The Zanadarian could not be certain that Tomar had discovered the secret cubicle all by himself; perhaps he had shared his discovery with another. . . .

He thought a moment, fingering the cold metal of the heavy dagger, then he knelt, tore open the throat of the lad's blouse, and cuffed him lightly but stingingly on the cheeks until the boy awoke from his swoon.

The youth lay unresistingly and stared at him in silence, a resolute expression on his features.

"Ah, Tomar, we meet again!" the Zanadarian laughed. "It was very clever of you to trace me to the secret cubicle. Tell me, did you discover my hiding place all by yourself or were there other minds to share the task—and, perhaps, the honor of finding me —eh?"

"I found you all by myself," said Tomar, stoutly— unaware that by so admitting he had just signed his own death warrant. Then the boy followed with a question of his own.

"Did you really push Captain Jandar overboard while we were taking on water supplies? Master Lukor and the others say you did, but I can't believe you would violate your own word of honor in so treacherous a fashion."

"You don't, eh?" Ulthar frowned, then laughed—an ugly sound, cold and hard and thick, with no humor in it. "Well, I shoved your heroic captain over the side with about as much compunction as you would show in treading on a serpent. Honor is a luxury desperate men cannot afford. It heartily amused me that Jandar was such a gullible fool as to accept my word or trust me in any fashion, but such emotions are common, I am told, among the lesser races. We gentlemen warriors of Zanadar reject your womanish concepts of honor and chivalry. This view of ours is a superior trait which sets us apart from the other, lower races of humankind on this world, and, in the end, it is the trait that will lead us to the mastery of the globe."

The boy continued to observe Ulthar with steady, fearless eyes during this speech. No emotion, except the faint shadow of revulsion, crosssed his features.

"Then, of course, you did not hesitate to mislead me with a pretence of friendship, so that you could betray that friendship and attempt to wreck the ship, when the first opportunity presented itself," the boy said tonelessly. The man shrugged, said nothing. The boy pressed him further.

"You must have been aware that I felt sympathy for you, and offered you in simple politeness an honest gesture of kindness. But instead of feeling gratitude, as a civilized gentleman would, you seized upon my youth and inexperience, idealism and gentility, as a tool to work your own murderous ends—or a weapon, to cut the throats of us all. As I suppose you are about to cut mine."

Ulthar of Zanadar sneered.

"What large words and noble sentiments for so small a boy-cub! Well, lad, you have me dead to rights, if it does you any good to know it. I would gladly lie—cheat—connive—or betray anyone, even myself, in order to stay alive and escape from my captivity."

"You could have forsworn your allegiance to Prince Thuton, you know," said Tomar. "You could have put your wits and courage, your knowledge and resourcefulness to the service of Shondakor and thus have risen high in her councils. Instead, you cling to a doomed way of life. For Zanadar will fall, you know."

Ulthar crooked an interrogative eyebrow.

"Hah! What, cub, you who prate of honor and chivalry, would urge me to betray my own people?"

"Yes, when they are wrong and we are right. For too long have the merciless Sky Pirates lived by looting and terrorizing the other civilizations of Thanator. It is no betrayal to realize an error and correct it, choosing the way of right over the way of evil and tyranny."

Something in the boy's clear, fearless tones, something in his steady, contemptuous eyes, something in his expression, perhaps scorn, touched Ulthar to the quick. The mockery left his features; his face went hard and ugly, his eyes cold and vicious.

"Enough fine words for now! You were right about one other thing, too. I *am* going to cut your throat, even as you guessed. And I think I'll do it now, if only to stop your sermon."

The boy regarded him unflinchingly.

"Do you mind if I take the blow standing on my feet and looking you in the face, rather than lying here like a trapped beast?" he asked contemptuously.

"Just as you like."

The boy got up, slowly, while Ulthar backed off toward the windows, watching him carefully. Then Tomar turned to face him and Ulthar closed in with the knife.

At that precise moment three things happened almost simultaneously.

First, the deck jolted under their feet—for at that moment Lukor had fired the catapult, sending the great steel arrow crunching into the ice peak, bringing the hurtling *Jalathadar* to a sudden halt.

The impact staggered the Zanadarian. He was thrust off balance, and his arms went out to the nearest stanchion to steady himself, and in that involuntary gesture his fingers loosened their hold on the dagger and it went flying.

Tomar staggered and almost fell himself, but steadied himself by grabbing hold of a wall bracket.

Regaining his balance with a sulphurous curse, Ulthar snatched the boy's rapier from his girdle and strode toward him, lamplight gleaming off the length of naked steel. Young Tomar watched the stealthy advance of the treacherous assassin. He knew he had not the slightest chance of opposing his young strength against the older man. Ulthar was taller, burlier, heavier than he—and was a master-swordsman. But the boy did not fancy the notion of standing supinely, waiting for his death blow. The blood of a thousand nobly born warrior ancestors clamored within him at that moment—bold men and gallant women who had stood and fought against overwhelming odds, rather than yield like slaves to the death blow.

So he snatched up the oil-lamp, still brightly burning in the wall bracket where Ulthar had set it, and threw it.

Startled, Ulthar raised his blade to knock the burning lamp aside. Instead, the thin glass of the lamp chimney shattered against the steel, drenching the Zanadarian from head to foot with black oil.

Burning black oil!

Within an instant, Ulthar was wrapped in flames. Uttering one great, horrible cry of surprise and rage and terror and pain, the flame-wrapped figure stumbled backward, flailing at burning body with burning hands—tripped over the window seat—hurled through the great bank of windows—and fell like a blazing meteor down to a sudden death on the frozen plains far below.

So perished Ulthar of Zanadar. With all the cruel cunning and treacherous ingenuity of which his cold, powerful intellect had been capable, he had labored mightily to destroy the *Jalathadar* and to frustrate it in its quest.

That he had ultimately failed was as much due to the quick thinking and steady nerves of a brave young boy as it was to the trickery of fate.

It was an hour or so later. The wind had fallen, and although the air was bitterly cold, the skies were clearing and the great, many-colored moons of Jupiter shone down on a scene of furious labor. They had seen many strange sights, those moons, in the innumerable aeons of time since their creation, but never one so bizarre as this.

Lashed securely to the utmost pinnacle of an ice mountain near the north pole of Callisto, a fantastic flying galleon hung aloft. Men wrapped in thick cloaks were cutting it free, chopping loose the great barbed arrow of steel that held it fast to the pinnacle, while other men labored mightily at repairing the damage to their vessel.

"Thanks to the Lords of Gordrimator," said Valkar, "the hull compartments were not breached when we slammed into the ice wall. We could have lost our supply of levitating gas and been marooned in the Frozen Land for the rest of our lives had that happened. As it was, we did not even spring one seam."

"Aye—and thanks to the bravery and cool head of young Tomar, here, our hidden enemy has been flushed from his lair and will trouble us no more," growled Lukor, tousling the boy's hair with rough affection.

Tomar was silent, his features pale, his manner withdrawn. He stood with the others on the poop, overlooking the workmen who were splicing together the shorn control cables with new cordage.

"It was a horrible way to die," the young man said finally.

"Death is always horrible because it is an end from which there can be no beginning again," observed Koja solemnly. "But in the case of the Zanadarian, the end was fitting. He would have slain us all by secret ways, by hidden treachery, sneaking from his concealed lair in the darkness. But you faced him bravely and fought cleanly and slew him honorably. You have nothing with which to reproach yourself, young Tomar."

The youth looked up at the impassive features and glittering eyes of the ungainly arthopode, and suddenly he smiled.

"I believe you are right, sir," he said.

And old Lukor laughed and took the youth by the nape of the neck and shook him lightly. The youth grinned at him.

"Ah, Tomar, you are a boy no longer. You have had your baptism of blood and fire and death younger than most of us, but you have come through it well, and you stand among us now, a man among men. Welcome!"

Valkar smiled, clapping the young man's shoulder. "I stand with Master Lukor on that, Tomar, but the next time you flush out a traitor from his hidey-hole, and finish him off single-handedly, try to kill him by some other manner than setting him afire. The laminated paper whereof the *Jalathadar* is constructed is highly flammable, you know, and it has always been Jandar's opinion that the gas stored under pressure in the double hull is as explosive as a gas called 'hydrogen' on his home world. You could have blown the ship apart, had it caught fire instead of Ulthar—"

He stopped, for Tomar had suddenly gone pale as paper and swayed on weak knees until Koja steadied him with a strong arm.

"Lords of Gordrimator!" gasped Tomar, feebly, "I never thought of that!"

They were still laughing a bit hysterically from the release of tension when grizzled old Haakon came puffing and blowing up to them, his heavy face red from exertion, wiping greasy hands on a bit of waste.

Valkar turned to greet him.

"What's the good news, Haakon?"

"Good news, indeed, captain!" the older man wheezed. "There's enough spare cable in the lockers to repair both wings and rudder stays, although they will not bear the full tension we could call on unsevered lines to take. A few days more work and, if we don't all freeze solid in this accursed land, we'll be on our way to Zanadar in good fashion—a little more beat up than we had intended to look, but able to fly well enough!"

Valkar yawned hugely and stretched until his joints creaked. "Good news is right, Haakon! Well, it's your watch. Me for my bed. The night has been long and busy. A few more nights so crowded with excitement, and I will give over adventuring and settle down to quiet days in Shondakor. Gentlemen?"

Lukor smothered a jaw-cracking yawn of his own.

"I'm for bed, too. Old bones tire easily, they say. What about you, friend Koja?"

The chitin-clad arthopode stared broodingly out over the moonlit ice fields. His tones were somber and sorrowful.

"I, too. But I am wondering where Jandar sleeps this night—if indeed he yet lives. And, in all our adventurings to come, if ever we will be able to find him in this world of foes. I had thought to stand beside him when we battled against the warriors of Zanadar, as we have fought many times ere this, he and I. Now, methinks I will fight alone . . . but I go to my soft bed, wondering where he slumbers tonight, under the many moons. . . ."

It was a question none of them could answer.

Book IV

GLADIATORS OF ZANADAR

Chapter 10

I MAKE A NEW FRIEND

We were taken out of the city of Narouk in the manner which I have already described, and, chained together in a long line, guarded by a dozen Perushtarian soldiers astride war-thaptors, we marched all that day into the hill country that lay northwest of the Bright Empire.

We had not been informed as to the nature of our fate or the place of our destination. If my companions in misfortune were aware of these matters, I, at least, was still ignorant of them. And during the long march I busied my mind with puzzling on the problem. It was as good a method as any for managing to forget the ache of weary muscles and the thirst that the clouds of gray road dust roused in me.

That we were being sent as sacrifices to some mysterious gods I strongly doubted, although I could not of course be certain. While I have learned much of the ways of the various races of Thanator, they still have secrets I have not yet penetrated, and one of these was the nature of their religion.

With the possible exception of the Sky Pirates of Zanadar, whose technological achievements are of such an extraordinary nature that they cannot be considered to stand at the same cultural level as the other natives of Thanator, those of the civilization I have thus far encountered in the course of my wanderings and adventures on this strange and curious world are generally at the level of the Bronze Age.

This is true, for example, of the Golden City of Shondakor, and it is true also of the bandit armies called the Black Legion. As for the Bright Empire of Perushtar, it reminds me most of some of the Semitic civilizations of Earth's antiquity—perhaps the Philistines or the Phoenicians or the Carthaginians.

As for Koja's own people, the warriors of the Yathoon Horde, that tremendous clan of nomad warriors who roam and rule the Great Plains of Haratha to the south, they are more akin to the Mongols or the Tartars, the ferocious and hardy men who rode at the heels of Genghis Khan and Tamerlane to whelm the gates of Europe with a flood of gore.

The puzzle came in at this point, for it is a truism of the study of history, that such civilizations, at least on my own native world, have always been dominated by powerful priesthoods. Organized religious hierarchies are found among all such early barbaric cultures, but this, simply, is not true of the races of Thanator.

Which is not to say the Thanatorians do not have their gods; they do, and they call them "the Lords of Gordrimator," Gordrimator being their name for the planet Jupiter, whose ocher-banded globe fills their night skies with its mighty shield.

But although the Thanatorians swear by these gods, they do not seem to worship them, or, if indeed they do, it is with rites and ceremonies so private that I have gone thus far in total ignorance of their very existence. For, in all my wanderings across the face of Callisto the Jungle Moon, never once have I discovered anything that resembled a temple or synagogue, shrine, or cathedral, and I have yet to encounter the

Callistan equivalent of priest, bonze, lama, or rabbi.*

And, while my adventures have so filled my time that I have never found sufficient leisure to explore the native literatures of Thanator as fully as my curiosity might desire, I have neither found nor heard of anything remotely like a sacred scripture or a prophetic book or even a volume of prayers or mantras. In short, the peoples of Thanator are as devoid of a formal religion as it is possible for any civilization to be.

The chances that we were bound for a bloody altar, to be slaughtered as offering to some savage god, was, therefore, highly unlikely. What was far more reasonable an explanation for the term "the Tribute" was that we were hostages en route to some warlike or savage tribe on the borders of the Bright Empire— a ransom paid in human lives for the safety of those borders. I knew little or nothing about the political situation in this distant corner of the world, but the explanation seemed likely. That meant, therefore, that with every step I was traveling further and further away from any chance at partaking in the raid on Zanadar and the rescue from captivity of the woman I loved.

Every two hours we were given a rest halt. We had a chance to relieve nature by the side of the road and

* Captain Dark seems to have forgotten his encounter with the wily and cunning priest of Hoom, devil-god of the Chac Yuul, as described in *Black Legion of Callisto*, the second volume of these chronicles. It is true, however, that this priest, Ool the Uncanny, was later revealed as one of the mysterious Mind Wizards of Kuur, who had seized a hold on the primitive, superstitious Black Legion warriors through his extraordinary mental powers. Thus unmasked as a false priest, his god a hoax, his cult a sham, Ool perhaps does not qualify as a genuine priest, which may be why Captain Dark omits reference to him in this passage.—L.C.

to restore our energy, for the guardsmen passed around oiled skins of sour-tasting but gloriously welcome water. Twice that long, endless day we were given food—slices of dried meat and huge chunks of coarse black bread, moistened with a little resinous wine. It was not the custom of the Perushtarians to starve or mistreat their slaves; we were, after all, worth money.

By nightfall we had penetrated very far into the hill country north of Ganatol and were now among the foothills of the White Mountains themselves. We made camp under the brilliant moons in a vast valley. The Perushtarian guardsmen had obviously made this journey before, and knew exactly what to do. Bonfires were lit in a huge circle. Stakes were driven deep into the soil in the center of this circle, and we slaves lay down on the earth to sleep, while the guards unrolled their pallets and took up guard stations about the bright-lit perimeter of the circle of fires. There was no opportunity to escape, and, in all candor, I was so exhausted from the all-day overland march that I fell asleep the instant I stretched out. We must have covered forty miles that day, and I have never walked so much in all my life.

The next day was an exact duplicate of the first, with the slight exception that it was even harder going. Every muscle in my body throbbed with agony and the effort to keep limping along took all of the manhood I could muster. Many of the slaves chained to us and bound for the Tribute could not keep up the pace. These were the old, the ill, the crippled, and a few surly types, doubtlessly discarded to join the Tribute because they were malingerers or troublemakers. Those who could not keep going were bundled on the pack-thaptors and rode in the rear. They received no food that night, and on the third day of the march, had learned to limp along somehow.

I began to think about my chances of escaping. Thus far we had been traveling more or less in the direction I secretly wanted to go, which was toward Zanadar. But surely at any time now we would be heading off in some other direction, and at that point I would want to make my attempt. On the third day of the march I began to keep my eyes open for an opportunity to get away. I watched the guards covertly, trying not to attract their attention. They were bored and rode along on their restive steeds, chatting and joking idly among themselves, not paying very much attention to we slaves.

Before long, I noticed that another man in the chain gang was doing much the same as I. Trudging along, his head down as if dispirited, he was sneaking covert glances to right and left, noting the bored and inattentive guards. He was a Perushtarian, with the bright, tomato-red skin of his people, and the bald head, but whereas most Perushtarians tend to run to fat, he was powerfully built, without an ounce of superfluous weight.

Although no taller than myself—he came up to my chin, in fact—the fellow had broad, sloping shoulders, sheathed in massive thews, powerful hands, and bowed but sturdy legs. He looked like a dwarfed Hercules, and his features, when I got a good look at them, appealed to me. For while he was a remarkably ugly man, with a broad, lipless slash of a mouth, a thick neck, and heavy, scowling brows, his eyes were quick and bright with intelligence, and there was an untamed truculence in the set of his grim jaw. In short, he looked like a good comrade to have on your side in a fight.

That night I contrived to get myself chained next to him. This was a simple matter. We were unchained to relieve ourselves and receive rations, and were chained again for sleeping in whatever sequence we had fallen into. I jostled my way next to him when the time came for the guards to snap the night chains on our slave collars. And I was correct in my guess as to the squat, powerful, ugly little man's intelligence. For he noticed what I did and shot me a thoughtful, searching glance from under scowling brows. I grinned frankly and openly back at him, as if to say "That's right—I did it deliberately."

While the guardsmen got us settled down for the night I let him look me over. He could see that I was healthy and fit and alert enough, and from my demeanor he could doubtless ascertain that I was not one of the many whose fighting manhood has been drained from them by the condition of servitude. Once the guards were bedded down, at some distance away, I spoke to him in a low tone, without moving my lips.

"You look strong. Are you strong enough to break these chains?"

"Maybe," he growled back. "You look like a man with some guts still left in you. Got enough to make a break for it, if we get a chance?"

I nodded. "My name is Darjan," I said.

"Mine is Ergon," he replied. "Where did you get that yellow hair?"

"From my mother," I said; then, with a glance at his bald bullet-head—"Where did you get yours'?"

He grinned, and with that grin I liked the man. For his ugly froglike face, which normally wore a sullen and truculent expression, lightened when he smiled, and humor sparkled in his eyes. I wondered who he was, and how he had kept his courage and humor and self-esteem during a lifetime of slavery. I longed to learn his story, but just then one of the guards yelled at us to stop talking, and we exchanged one silent grin, rolled over, and slept.

The next day we were chained together and managed to converse in low tones during the long march, while the inattentive guards were not near.

I discovered that Ergon had, as I had first surmised, been born to slavery, but had been raised in an indulgent household by a master considerably more kind and humane than the normal run of slavekeepers in the Bright Empire.

He was not a native of Narouk at all, it seemed, but had been born in the capital of the Bright Empire itself, the city of Glorious Perusht, as they call it, on the island of the same name, amid the waters of the Corund Laj. The kindly master in whose household he had grown up was named Idolon. He must have been a curious oddity among the greedy, gold-hungry oligarchs of Perushtar, for he was more philosopher than merchant, and, although a remarkably wealthy man, more interested in adding to his superb collection of rare books than to the coins in his coffers.

This lord Idolon, it seemed, regarded the institution of slavery as a barbarity unworthy of a genuine civilization. In that opinion he must have been truly alone among his fellow merchant princes. At any rate, while he did not quite dare risk offending against caste and tradition by freeing his slaves, he encouraged them to consider themselves as the equals of free men, and to resist the spirit-sapping and dehumanizing degradations of their sorry state.

He did not last very long, it seems. A coalition of Perushtarian merchant lords ruined him, and drove him into bankruptcy, whereupon his possessions—including his slaves—went on the auction block. But

Ergon, then a youth, remembered lord Idolon and did not take well to being resold. He escaped and, before being recaptured, managed to assassinate three of the five conspirators who had destroyed his master. Only his value as human merchandise prevented his captors from executing him. He was resold into Narouk, became the property of the House of Ildth, and underwent training as a public gladiator, due to his remarkable strength. But he proved sullen and unruly, and was sent many times to the whipping post for his infractions against the rules of his servitude. On the last such occasion he turned on his tormentor, broke his chains—and the neck of the man who wielded the whip. Since the Tribute had fallen on lord Cham that month, his owners, unwilling to tolerate such a dangerous man in the midst of their generally spineless collection of human cattle, sold him off at a low price to the Iskelions.

Having learned Ergon's story, I told him my own—or, at least, a heavily censored version of it, which avoided any mention of my birth on another planet and my adventures against the Black Legion or the Sky Pirates. I explained to Ergon that my homeland lay far away, that I had been a wandering mercenary swordsman until I ended up at the slave wheels of a Zanadarian galleon, from which the treachery of a false friend had precipitated me into the waters of the Corund Laj. He grinned at this rather mysteriously.

"I rejoice to learn the House of Iskelion preserves the remnants of a sense of humor among their many possessions," he growled. "The Zanadarians, I trust, will appreciate the jest as well!"

"The Zanadarians? I don't understand you. What are you talking about?"

"Why, the Tribute, Darjan. What do you think I am

talking about? You know we are both part of this month's Tribute, do you not?"

I confessed I was aware of it. He shrugged, as if the connection was self-explanatory.

"Well, then," he grunted.

"I'm afraid I still don't get the point of the joke," I admitted. "To tell the truth, I really don't know anything about the Tribute. I have heard the term several times, but everybody seems to take it for granted that the meaning is obvious, and no one has yet bothered to explain it to me."

He regarded me with blank amazement.

"Do you mean to say you don't know where you are going?"

"I mean just that," I said. "I assume—without any particular reason behind the assumption—that we are a sort of human ransom being sent to buy off some savage border tribe who would otherwise harass the caravans of Narouk. But what tribe or nation that may be, I have no notion."

Ergon began to laugh.

"The caravans of Narouk would indeed be harassed, were not the Tribute paid," he grunted. "Not by any 'savage border tribe,' but by a rapacious fleet dispatched by the Sky Pirates of Zanadar!"

My jaw fell, my cheeks crimsoned, and I feel certain I presented an expression of slack-jawed idiocy as Ergon's words and their import penetrated my skull.

"You cannot mean—"

"But certainly," he growled. "Where else would the Tribute be bound for, if not to Zanadar, the City in the Clouds?"

Chapter 11

THE CITY IN THE CLOUDS

Even had I still wished to make a break with Ergon, the last opportunity to do so had escaped us. For within the hour we were herded off the road to a rounded knoll barren of trees or other encumbrances. Then, while I watched with a mingling of emotions I give my reader free rein to imagine for himself, there descended upon us from the sky a gigantic ornithopter.

Obviously, we had been bound for this rendezvous all along. The humor inherent in the situation would have been almost enjoyable, had not my predicament been so hazardous. For I had been stealthily scrutinizing the roadside by some chance to escape from my captivity and had been busy striking up acquaintances with promisingly burly-shouldered fellow slaves in order to make my way to Zanadar in time to assist in the rescue of the Princess Darloona—when all the time, unknown to myself, I was being safely and carefully escorted to Zanadar itself. It was really very funny, when you looked at it that way.

The abruptness with which we were met by the transport galleon relieved me of a possible embarrassment. For how could I possibly have explained to Ergon that I no longer desired to make my escape with him or anyone else? I have no doubt the surly, suspicious fellow would either have considered me mad or a sort of *agent provocateur*, planted by the Perushtarian oligarchate to nose out mutiny and disaffection among the slaves.

As it was, however, the opportunity we were awaiting simply did not present itself in time, so we had to abandon our planned escape and await what the future would bring.

The Zanadarian vessel that descended to take aboard the Tribute was not a frigate such as were the *Jalathadar* and the *Kajazell**—where they had the slim, sharp lines of a striking hawk, this vessel—the *Huronoy* was its name—had the portly, lumbering, rotund look of a freighter—which is exactly what it turned out to be.

It is a tricky matter, maneuvering the weightless ornithopters into anything resembling a landing, and whoever was in charge of the *Huronoy* on this voyage, certainly knew his business, for he brought the lumbering freighter down to take aboard his human cargo with a deft ease that was all the more admirable when you recall the fierce and unpredictable up-drafts that plague navigation over this rugged country.

Large double doors opened in the hull. A gangplank descended, and we were herded up it in a double line, while bored Naroukian guardsmen numbered us off and a bewhiskered and very piratical-looking Zanadarian skipper checked over his bill of lading. As there was just the slightest chance that some member of the crew might have recognized me by my unique combination of fair skin, blue eyes, and straw-blond hair, from my earlier visit to the City in the Clouds,

---

* Captain Dark refers to the flagship of Prince Thuton's fleet, among whose wheel slave-gangs he and the Yathoon chieftain, Koja, served briefly for one voyage, as described in *Jandar of Callisto*, the first book of these adventures.—L.C.

I had already taken the precaution of affecting some slight disguise to hamper recognition. I had, in fact, done so just as soon as we were brought up the rounded knoll and the *Huronoy* came into view aloft.

It was not a very effective disguise; however, I did not think I would arouse any notice or suspicion by donning it. Many of my fellow-slaves, during the long trek, had covered their heads or faces with scraps of cloth torn from their garments, in order to avoid breathing in the gray dust that rose in choking clouds around us as we trudged that long and dusty road. I had merely torn off a thick strip of cloth from the bottom of my tunic and wound it about my brows so that it concealed my yellow thatch, leaving one end dangling loose, which could be drawn to cover my face upon need, as I drew it when Ergon and I were being taken up the gangplank.

No one noticed—or, at least, no one that mattered. For I saw that Ergon turned a puzzled, questioning glance upon me as I covered my face. The rude disguise should have been sufficient to conceal my identity. As for the clear bronze tan of my skin, there was nothing I could do to disguise that, and luckily it was not so remarkably different from the norm as were my yellow locks. The Thanatorians differ very greatly in their variety of skin colors, from the swarthiness of the Chac Yuul, the papery-whiteness of the Zanadarians, the tawny amber of the Ku Thad, and the brilliant scarlet of the Perushtarians. But intermarriage beween these ethnic groupings is far from unusual: Lukor and the people of his city of Ganatol, for example, represent an off shoot of halfbreeds born to marriages between members of the Zanadarian and Chac Yuul groups—and many shades and tones and variations of coloring are commonly found among the lower classes of each civilization, so I hoped my tan skin would pass scrutiny.

The cargo hold was capacious, if not exactly a model of luxury. Stretched out beside the sullen Ergon, I contemplated my future in a rather dismal mood. It seemed most likely that during the several days of my captivity since Ulthar had tipped me overboard, the *Jalathadar* would have completed its mission. By now, surely, my comrades had either failed or succeeded in the desperate attempt to rescue Darloona from the stronghold of the villainous Prince Thuton. By now, Valkar, Koja, Lukor, and the others were either on their return voyage to Shondakor with the princess, or in their graves or the prison cells of Zanadar. Either way, my position looked hopeless from all I could tell. I would reach Zanadar safely, that I knew, but too late to join my comrades in victory or die beside them in defeat.

Chained in the hold, I saw nothing of the capital of the Sky Pirates when we descended ere long to a landing in the docks. We were led out across the long quays of hewn stone, scoured by a merciless wind that whipped rock dust in our eyes. I had one brief glimpse of soaring pylons and impregnable fortress walls before my captors plunged me again into gloom, this time the gloom of the slave pens. We were led to troughs of water and told to remove as much of the road dust from our persons as we could, then we were led to the block in a huge echoing room where several important-looking officials awaited our coming to apportion us to our tasks.

Slaves are not bought and sold in Zanadar, they are assigned.

The younger of the men examining us was a hard-faced, cold-eyed young man with a pallid, greasy, unhealthy complexion, nattily dressed in vivid silk pajamas and gauntlets sewn with brilliant gems. He was not impressed with our appearance.

"A sorry-looking lot, Thon," he observed. "Just look at them. Half of them are toothless grandfathers ready for the grave, the others either drooling cretins or hollow-chested invalids dying from the coughing fever. Narouk must learn to do better than this, or the Council of Captains may level a punitive expedition against the city."

The man he had addressed as Thon was a barrel-chested, hearty-looking man in his middle forties, graying at the temples, with a firm jaw and an air of command about him. He wore a simple leather tunic, greaves and girdle, and a large hooded cloak of bottle-green. The gaily dressed aristocrat who surveyed us with such high-bred scorn pressed a pomander ball to his nostrils as if to alleviate some fancied stench.

"Well, one or two of them look likely enough material," Theon said gruffly, singling out both Ergon and myself with his eyes. "Yonder dog with the tan skin has a good physique, and the red-skin at his side would make a good mace-man. I'll take those two and you can have your pick of the rest, my lord."

"How like you, Thon, to pick out the likeliest of the lot for your precious corps," sniffed the one in silk pajamas. "I like the looks of the tan-skinned oaf myself—he stands tall and has an air of breeding about him. A touch of the gelding wire to cow his spirits, and he would make a rather handsome servant."

My blood ran cold at his words. The most horrible thing about it all was not so much what he said, although God knows that was grim enough, but the negligent, casual manner in which he said it. It was as if he was discussing some dumb animal, not a human being like himself.

The older man shrugged.

"Mayhap, my lord. But my need takes priority over your requirements. For the prince will have his entertainments, as you know, and I am short two good men."

The languid young man waved his pomander ball with a disdainful small *moue* of pique.

"Oh, very well, take them. I will have to make do with the best of what is left, I suppose. . . ."

The burly, graying man exchanged a few curt words with the clerks, scribbled something on a roll of parchment, affixed a seal ring to dripping wax, and led both Ergon and me apart from the others. My Perushtarian friend glanced at me with a grunt of satisfaction.

"Well, Darjan, at least we will still be together!"

"Yes," I nodded. "And perhaps we can still arrange an escape—"

"No talking, you two," one of the guards growled, cuffing me lightly alongside the head. "Step lively, now. The gamesmaster is a busy man and does not like to be kept waiting."

Our new owner was Gamesmaster of Zanadar, which meant he was in charge of the management of the great arena and supervisor of the spectacles and entertainments performed there regularly. For the Zanadarians, much like the Romans before them, delight in sport, and there is no sport more exciting than men fighting for their lives. This was to be our fate, it seemed.

Our quarters lay beneath the great arena itself, which lay at one end of the city, beneath an enormous dome of crystal panes in a natural cuplike depression

in the rock, perhaps the crater of a long-extinct vol-
cano. A virtual labyrinth of tunnels and passages,
rooms and suites and cubicles, had been hollowed out
of the soft, lavalike rock below the sandy floor of the
arena. There the trained fighting men and the ferocious beasts against which they were pitted were kept.

Our training began almost immediately. Gamesmaster Thon interviewed us briefly to form an estimate
of our skills. I told him I was an excellent swordsman,
but, oddly enough, he frowned at this and did not
seem at all pleased with the news. I later learned that
sword fights are not given in the arena for two reasons.
For one thing, they are not very spectacular. The spectators in the top tiers demand something a little more
active and exciting than watching two men standing
face to face flickering thin steel blades at each other.

The other reason is that a slave armed with a sword
is a dangerous man and might well slay his guards
and attempt an escape.

So, instead of a sword I was given a spear and sent
to train with the other *keraxians,* or spearmen. There
was not much chance of a slave armed with a spear
running amok or making a break for freedom. The
spears we used were Harathian weapons, such as
those employed by the Yathoon huntsmen of the
southern plains. They are fifteen feet long, shod in
heavy bronze, and cumbersome as well as awkward.

Because of his burly shoulders and deep chest, my
friend Ergon was assigned to the *tharians,* or ax-men,
who fight with the enormous bronze double-bladed
mace, which is the weapon of choice among a people
known as the Kumalians. One needed to have iron
thews to employ such a weapon, for the Kumalian
mace weighs thirty pounds and, including the shaft,
measures nearly five feet in length.

We saw very little of each other, Ergon and I, in the next few days, because our trainers kept us busy from dawn to dark, and our labors were exhausting. The reason for this accelerated program was that we were to fight in the very next games, which were only a few days away. The Zanadarians are a cruel, lusty people who love fighting and vastly enjoy seeing men pitted in a desperate struggle against savage beasts or sometimes even more savage men and any excuse for the games is valid in their eyes. These particular games, for example, were being held for no more reason than an expected eclipse in which two of the Jovian satellites were to meet in a rare conjunction. On the night of the "great games," as the festival of death was called, Ramavad would be eclipsed behind Imavad.

Ramavad, or Europa, is a luminous globe of frosty azure-silver, while Imavad, or Ganymede, is a deep crimson. The symbolism is obvious: in the peculiar mysticism of the Thanatorians, Ramavad represents the purity and holiness of life, while Imavad stands for blood and death and destruction. And the games to be held on this night of blood would be, I was told, appropriately sanguinary.

The training given us *keraxians* was simple, but, I trusted, effective. The great black *jaruka*-wood spears were all we would have wherewith to fight our adversaries, and the trouble was we could not be certain in advance as to which of the dreadful predators of the Callistan jungles we would be set against.

The consensus of opinion among the other *keraxians* of my team was that we would be sent out to fight a pride of savage deltagars. The deltagar may be described as a twenty-foot-long supertiger with scarlet fur and a lashing, whiplike tail edged with jagged serrations or horny blades. The beast is noted for his ferocity even among the terrible monstrosities of this Jungle Moon, and much to my surprise my fellow gladiators did not seem to regard the deltagar as a particularly vicious opponent. This, I found out, was due to the fact that while a furious fighter, the deltagar can indeed be slain by such spears as we would be armed with, as only a coat of fur protected its vital organs from our bronze blades.

My fellow *keraxians* would have been most uneasy had they thought they might be sent out against yathribs, for these are far more dangerous and not so easily killed with spears. Yathribs are dragon cats of the Grand Kumala, whose rippling, steely-thewed catlike bodies are armored in glittering emerald scales, which pale to tawny yellow at the belly plates. Their feet are armed with slashing bird claws, and a row of jagged spines runs down their tails to the lashing tip. Being more reptilian than mammalian, and sheathed in tough, flexible scales, they are considerably harder to kill than deltagars.

I, frankly, burst into cold perspiration at the thought of fighting against either brute, armed only with a wooden spear. A bazooka or a satchel of fragmentation grenades would have been my choice had I been consulted in the matter.

In time I did get a chance to compare notes with my partner in misfortune, Ergon. We encountered each other on the third day of our training, when we were being drilled in the ceremonial march around the vast bowl-shaped stadium. During a rest period, I sauntered over to where he squatted and clapped him affectionately on the shoulder. He grinned up at me, his froglike face gleaming with perspiration. In this strange theater of death, among hosts of strangers, it was good to find a friend you knew.

"How are the *keraxians?*" he inquired. "I understand you will be set against a pride of deltagars brought hither from the jungle country."

"So the barracks gossip has it," I replied. "And how are things among the *tharians?* What manner of beast will you be fighting?"

"The prevailing opinion among my peers is that they will send vastodons against us," he said, naming the great elephant boar of the jungles. The brute has the slate-gray leathery hide of the terrestrial pachyderm, but the head more closely resembles that of the wild boar, with its little pig-eyes, coarse black bristles, long, prehensile snout, and blunt, vicious tusks. They are wicked fighters and dangerous because, while large and heavy, they are also very fast and charge like lightning. I commiserated with him.

"And, as for the rest of your query," he grimaced, rubbing his shoulder muscles, "things are about as usual among the *tharians*. The maces we are armed with seem to grow heavier every day, and I am discovering muscles I did not even know I possessed. I discover them chiefly," he said in wry tones, "when they begin to ache!"

I laughed. He was regarding me with a curious expression in his eyes.

"You have taken to covering your hair, I see," he remarked.

"Why, yes, Ergon. No particular reason, except that everyone seems to find my yellow hair so unusual that, just to spare further questions as to my homeland, I have adopted this mode of headgear," I said. The fact of the matter was that I went in deadly fear of being recognized. Many of the members of Prince Thuton's court visited the training fields to watch us work out,

and I feared lest one of these sports buffs might recognize me from my earlier exploits here in the City in
the Clouds. So I had adopted a light linen headdress,
similar to that worn of old by the Pharaohs of Egypt,
which covered my hair and shaded my eyes to make
their blueness less noticeable. I had explained this unusual hair-covering as one worn by ancient custom
among my people, and the spearmaster had no reasons to refuse me this small courtesy.

Ergon smiled rather cryptically, but said nothing.

Then he dropped his bombshell.

"Among my team members there are several that
once served among the Chac Yuul," he said casually.
"They relate a marvelous account to explain how the
Black Legion was driven forth from the city of Shondakor the Golden, and in particular they are full of
stories about a remarkable adventurer with yellow
hair and blue eyes and light skin, a fellow named
Jandar."

I cleared my throat. "Oh?"

"Yes. According to them, this Jandar is a singularly
heroic fellow. Disguised as a mercenary swordsman,
formerly in service to one of the Perushtarian Seraans,
he entered Shondakor alone when it was in the hands
of the Black Legion, joined the legion and worked
his way up to a position of command and single-
handedly rescued the Princess Darloona from a forced
marriage with the despicable son of the chief warlord
of the Black Legion.*"

"These things are always exaggerated in the telling,"
I said, with a poor semblance of indifference.

"Oh, doubtless," smiled Ergon. "This Darloona, by

* Readers will find the whole story of this particular adventure
related in a book called *Black Legion of Callisto*, the second
volume in these chronicles.—L.C.

the way, is the same young woman who is now held prisoner here in Zanadar, and upon whom Prince Thuton is pressing his suit. Like most other leaders, Prince Thuton refuses to learn a lesson from past history, evidently. For the story runs that this Jandar is still alive, and if I were in Prince Thuton's place, I would carefully avoid forcing a marriage upon this Princess Darloona. For the last time she was in such a position, this Jandar fellow overthrew the entire Black Legion to free her. To one who has already conquered the Black Legion, the Sky Pirates themselves should not prove very difficult an obstacle to overcome."

I looked steadily into his eyes, abandoning all pretence of indifference.

"Just what is it that you are trying to say, Ergon?" I asked quietly.

He smiled. "Nothing, really. Except that I keep my mouth closed on the secrets of those few whom I call my friends. And one thing more . . ."

"What is that?"

"If this Jandar should happen to make an appearance here in Zanadar, by any chance, I would be proud to stand at his side with naked steel in my hands and fight against his foes. To the death, friend Darjan. To the death!"

Then the guards came, marshaling us into ranks again, and I had no opportunity to reply to his vow. But we did exchange one long, deep look, into each other's eyes, and when we parted, my heart felt somewhat lightened.

For in my coming battle, I now had at least one ally.

Chapter 12

THE FESTIVAL OF DEATH

As well as Ergon of Perusht, I had one other friend in
Zanadar, and that was one of my fellow *keraxians,* a
warrior named Zantor. He was a native-born Zanadarian, with the papery-white skin and lank hair and
jet-black eyes of his race. A towering broad-shouldered
giant of a man was Zantor, and a man of brooding
sorrow and grim, sullen moods.

He had once been one of the Sky Pirates. In fact, he
had been a great chieftain among the Captains of the
Clouds, as the corsair princes of Zanadar are known.
At the helm of his galleon, the *Xaxar*—"the Terror"—
he had been famed among the Sky Pirates as much for
his phenomenal good fortune as for his unusual traits,
for among the cruel and rapacious sky hawks of Zanadar, it was Zantor alone who had a sense of honor and
chivalry, a dislike for the indiscriminate shedding of
blood, and a stern sense of justice, tempered with
mercy.

From this position of high repute he had at length
fallen, and his fall was due in large measure to this
gentler side of his nature. For he had unwisely objected to the brutal slaughter of three hundred rebellious slaves during an uprising in the arena slave pens
only six months before. He had dared criticize the
justice of Prince Thuton himself and had petitioned

him for mercy on behalf of the slaves. For this gesture
of civilized restraint, Thuton had cynically stripped
him of all rank and honor, chaining him among the
arena slaves, with the cynical observation that if Zantor so bemoaned the death of the rebels, he was welcome to die among them.

But Zantor had not died. He had fought against
savage men and wild beasts thirteen times in the great
games of Zanadar, and each time he had survived the
ordeal among the victors. For this he had become
something of a hero even to the Sky Pirates themselves, who would otherwise, taking their cue from the
attitude of their prince, have despised him as a milky-
livered coward. But even the cruel Captains of the
Clouds could not but feel admiration for so mighty a
fighting man as Zantor. In all the annals of Zanadar,
he was the only gladiator in a thousand years to have
fought bare-handed against a ferocious bull yathrib,
slaying the monster, and surviving to tell the tale.

While most of his former friends ridiculed him for
what they considered his unmanly concern for the
lives of slaves which were, after all, mere human cattle, and delighted in his fall from favor, the dignity
with which Zantor had comported himself during his
new career in the arena and the remarkable bravery
and prowess he had displayed had won him many
admirers—much to the annoyance of Prince Thuton
and his sycophantic courtiers.

I at first regarded Zantor with some revulsion myself and rebuffed his overtures of friendship with a
certain coolness. Even a Sky Pirate fallen from favor
and condemned to death in the arena is still a Sky
Pirate, I reasoned, and partook of the collective guilt
of his people. But Zantor's quiet dignity won me to
reluctant admiration in time, and, as well, I learned

from the other arena slaves that when he had been one of the great corsair captains, Zantor of the *Xaxar* had been noted for his generosity, his concern for the fighting men under his command, and the restraint and mercy he commonly displayed toward all those he defeated in battle. At length, reflecting that few men can help adopting the standards of the society into which they are born and that even among the cruel and rapacious Sky Pirates, Zantor had somehow learned the gentler traits of civilized humanity, I warmed toward him, regretting my former rebuffs. We became fast freinds.

From my new comrades, I learned much concerning those topics whose importance was uppermost in my mind. The Princess Darloona, I discovered, to my hearty relief, was still unwed, although Prince Thuton had exerted much pressure to win her hand, threatening a full-scale attack against her kingdom if she continued to resist his suit. I also inquired carefully and unobtrusively as to the *Jalathadar*. By any count, the aerial galleon should have launched its attack against the City in the Clouds many days before. To my astonishment, I learned that this had not happened. No one whom I queried had heard the slightest rumor of a captive vessel being employed against Zanadar in a Trojan Horse maneuver—and the grapevine among the slaves of the Sky Pirates is a most highly developed intelligence network. If Prince Thuton so much as got a headache from too heartily imbibing in the fruit of the vine, precise details were commonly available to every slave in the city within the hour. Had any such attack been launched—had even a patrol ornithopter encountered and given battle to or destroyed such a vessel in the vicinity—it would have been common knowledge.

My heart sank with despair. I could only conclude from this that the expedition had somehow come to grief after the treachery of Ulthar precipitated me into the waves of the Corund Laj. With so cunning and patient a Judas aboard, it was easy enough to see how the *Jalathadar* could have been downed. Perhaps it had collided with a mountain peak during the hours of darkness; perhaps it had been carried off course into the frozen north, there to meet a lonely doom among the ice plains. Whatever had been the fateful end of the gallant expedition, I mourned the loss of my friends and faced the future with grim foreboding.

Now I alone was left to aid my beloved princess. And there seemed little enough that I, a slave condemned to die in the great arena, could do to free her from the clutches of Prince Thuton. It looked as if my long and adventurous odyssey was coming to an end at last, and that Darloona's last frail hope for freedom would perish before her eyes in the festival of death.

The day came at last. We were given a light but hearty meal of excellent steak and strong red wine, and, garbed in fighting-harness, we trooped forth into the vast amphitheater to fight for our lives.

It was a brilliant day. The smoothly raked sands of the arena were bathed in floods of daylight. Above us arched the clear, sparkling glass panes of the enormous geodesic dome that shielded the throng from the bitterly cold winds blowing at this height. Tier on tier of benches, ringed in the arena floor like the bleachers of some barbaric football stadium, were crowded with a sea of faces, for most of the lords and nobles of Zanadar and their women had turned out in their holiday finery to watch us fight and die this day for their pleasure.

The royal box was only a few tiers above the retaining wall that encircled the floor of the arena and protected the audience from the savage beasts, the rebellious slaves, or both. There, enthroned in a cushioned chair beneath a canopy of sky-blue silk, Prince Thuton lolled at ease, a coldly handsome young man with cynical, indifferent, hooded eyes and a cruel mouth.

At his side sat Darloona!

My heart stopped as I saw her. It had been so long since last I had looked upon her ripe loveliness. Although her face had haunted my dreams through an endless succession of nights and days, the sight of her choked the breath in my throat and brought moisture to my eyes. She was so very beautiful. The weeks of her imprisonment had not dimmed the radiance of her slanting emerald eyes nor tarnished the sunset glory of her red-gold mane, nor had they daunted her proud, courageous spirit. She sat icily aloof, next to Thuton's cushioned chair, but apart from him in queenly isolation. Her head was high, her expression inscrutable, her mouth stubborn. How much I loved her at that moment! Gladly would I have laid down my life to set her free from her despicable imprisonment, but, alas, it seemed the mocking Fates would have me spend my heart's blood on the baking sands of the arena, locked in futile and meaningless struggle with some jungle beast and all for the callous amusement of the cruel, blood-lusting Zanadarians.

Thon the Gamesmaster, in a gilded chariot drawn by a superb matched team of rare snow-white thaptors, led us on full parade as the games commenced. We trudged the entire circuit of the amphitheater twice, saluted before the royal box, receiving a negligent wave of Thuton's bejeweled hand. Then we retired to the pits beneath the arena as the festivities began in earnest.

First came the chariot races, in which champions selected from four teams vied with each other for the prize of a gold chaplet which Thuton would bestow on the victor. In this contest, the Royal Blues were the favorite, although the Reds and the Silvers were close contenders for second place. The Zanadarians found enormous excitement in chariot races, as had the Romans and the Byzantines of my own world, and the grandstands were divided into parties of those who favored each color. Indeed, as Glykon of the Blues, champion of the team favored by most, entered the arena the cheers and applause were so thunderous some feared the glass dome that sheltered the stands from the frigid winds would crack from the rebounding echoes.

The chariot races filled up most of the morning. With noon, the audience munched picnic lunches or purchased food from vendors who hawked their wares through the aisles. And, with their food, the Zanadarians liked a little fresh-spilled blood for sauce, so the first gladiators emerged from the Gate of Heroes, as the barred portal was called, to do battle for their noontime pleasure.

There were, as I have said, two varieties of gladiatorial combat, the *keraxians,* or spearmen, and the *tharians,* who were armed with axes. Those of us who were arena slaves were considered mere games fodder, good for little more than a gory death. But there were star gladiators among us who occupied a privileged position in the games—mighty champions, each of whom had his own particular following and his own colors. Zantor was the only one of these I knew personally, for they were a snobbish lot and enjoyed special privileges. They had their own private suites of apartments in the pits, instead of bunking in the common barracks with the rest of us, and it was amusing in a way to see them strutting about in gilt breastplates, greaves, and plumed helms, with all the arrogance of conquerors, although, they were slaves and really no different from the rest of us. Some of them, however, such as Prince Thuton's pet, Panchan, lived in apartments of sumptuous and silken luxury, dined off gourmet delicacies sent from the Prince's own table on plates of precious metal, had female slaves for their own pleasure, and lived bedecked with gems as if they were princes themselves.

This Panchan was the greatest of the champions, and was reckoned a superb swordsman. I have said that the Sky Pirates feared to arm the arena slaves with weapons less cumbersome than spears or maces, and this is true. Panchan was the sole exception to this rule. He was a surly, girlishly handsome young giant with a magnificently developed golden body he liked to display to the admiring throng. Where most gladiators sensibly protected themselves with cuirass, greaves, gauntlets, helm, and mail skirt, this golden young god of the great games fought nearly naked, wearing but sandals, a browband to keep his abundant mane out of his eyes, and a narrow strip of scarlet silk wound about his loins. The crowd adored him and Thuton had several times offered him his freedom after a particularly brilliant victory, but Panchan preferred the idolatry of the arena to the dubious hazards of freedom. To him alone was given the rare honor of dispatching his victims with a rapier.

Although none of us could stand Panchan for his sneering airs of supercilious superiority and the effeminate luxury in which he lived, he was, to do him justice, a great fighting man and well deserved the admiration his prowess had earned him. For he was one of the few gladiators who could use spear or ax with equal dexterity. Sometimes, during the grand mêlée which generally crowned the evening of the games, he fought with the *keraxians*, other times, with the *tharians*—always he displayed the adroit facility and graceful agility of form that marked him as a great champion. There had developed considerable rivalry between him and my new friend Zantor, however. No one quite knew how this rivalry had gotten started in the first place, although perhaps it began, quite simply, because Zantor was free-born and a former master-corsair of the realm, while Panchan, for all his champion status, had been born a lowly arena slave.

Or Panchan's hatred of Zantor might have been caused by the merely human fear of a successful rival. For when Zantor had first entered in the arena, he had been booed and hissed, but before long his great courage and dignity and fighting skills had won him the applause of the fickle throng, until by now his popularity rivaled that of Panchan himself. At any rate, Zantor had been trained to fight in my own team, the *keraxians*, and from his first appearances in the ranks of the gladiatorial spearmen, Panchan had fought with the *tharians* exclusively. The two rivals had fought in personal contests many times, but always Zantor, although an older and heavier man, had managed to hold his own against the spoiled, sullen, golden young god of the games. Which, doubtless, had added fresh poison to the rancor in Panchan's heart.

With noon, as I said earlier, the gladiatorial contests began. The first of these were team battles, in which six or eight *keraxians* were pitted against an equal number of *tharians*.

None of the famous champions of either team deigned to partake in these opening engagements, which were in the nature of warm-up exercises anyway, and which consisted of hastily trained arena slaves who were quite expendable. But I noticed Zantor in the sidelines, carefully observing how his teammates fought and urging us on with his counsel as much as by the heartening influence of his presence.

I fought in three of the six opening contests and managed to acquit myself decently. The spear has never been my weapon, but I had learned enough of its use to defend myself quite adequately. And defend myself is about all I did, I must confess. I am perfectly willing to fight and to kill in defense of my own life and honor and to protect my friends and loved ones, but it sickened me to seek the acclaim of the throng by murdering a man who has done me no harm and whom I cannot consider my enemy. So I merely defended myself against the ax men who were pitted against me and did not seek to slay them. My opponents in general seemed to feel the same way about the matter, and once they learned I had no intention of striving to strike through the weak places in their defense, we merely exchanged blows until the Gamesmaster terminated the contest.

The afternoon was well advanced by this time, and the rather lackluster performance of these opening contests bored the crowd, who began booing us lustily and even, in some cases, pelting us with scraps of food from their lunches. Noting the restive nature of the throng, the Gamesmaster decided to change his schedule and set forth a grand mêlée before any of the garbage began being tossed his way. The mêlée, usually reserved for the final act of the games, is a great favorite with the Zanadarians and resembles a full-scale mock battle. Perhaps I should explain at this point that the great games generally last three or four days and feature a carefully balanced variety of entertainment. The first day, as I have described already, begins traditionally with chariot racing and continues with hand-to-hand combat between teams randomly selected from among the novice *keraxians* and *tharians*, ending, in early evening, with the grand mêlée. On the second day, the more expert members of both gladiatorial teams are pitted against wild beasts, either singly or *en masse;* the third day, which usually terminates the games, features the personal contests of the champions, after a sequence of gory warm-up exercises in which each champion gets a chance to slaughter as many of the expendable arena slaves as he likes.

For the mêlée we were ranked in opposed hosts under a great show of banners and pennons emblazoned with the mock heraldries of imaginary or mythical cities. With much flourishing of trumpets, we charged. Unlike the opening contests, the mêlée was a serious affair in which each team or side was encouraged, under threat of death, to slaughter as many opponents as possible. Nonetheless, I still fought in the main to protect myself and kept rather close to the leader of my side, Zantor. My reason for doing so was a rumor which had reached my ears—a rumor that Panchan, on the express command of Prince Thuton, had vowed to slay his rival during the personal combat of the leaders of the hosts which was the ultimate highpoint of the entire affair.

And he had sworn to kill him "by fair means or by foul," the rumor whispered. Well, Zantor and Ergon were the two best friends I had found here in Zanadar, and I was determined to do what I could to prevent treachery. I regarded my life as a thing of little importance at this low ebb of my fortunes. I would die, undoubtedly, at some point during these interminable bloody shows, and if die I must, I would prefer it be in a worthy cause.

To my mind there are few causes in life more worthy than friendship.

Keeping close to Zantor's back, I fought my way through the mass of tangled, battling gladiators and spotted Ergon heading for me through the mêlée. I caught his eye and grinned and was somewhat surprised to see him plow directly for me with grim purposefulness. Surely, he did not mean to engage me. Although we fought on opposite sides, our friendship was such that neither of us would wish to engage the other in combat. I concluded he must have some special reason for seeking me out on this mock battlefield, and thus instead of avoiding the conflict, as I would otherwise have done, I permitted him to approach.

The ugly little Perushtarian swung his mace to engage and turn aside my spear—using, I noticed, the *flat* of the blade, rather than the edge, which might have snapped the shaft of my weapon, leaving me defenseless. Then, ducking under the spear, he dropped his mace and caught me in the bear hug of a wrestler.

As he did this he hissed loudly in my ear that we should fake a tussle. Wonderingly, I slipped out of his grasp, caught his bald bullet-head in the crook of my arm, and pretended to be strangling him violently.

"What in the world is all this about, Ergon?" I whispered.

"You are good friends with your team leader, the champion Zantor, are you not?" he inquired in a hoarse mutter. I nodded. He continued: "Well, that pretty boy, Panchan, is boasting how he's going to mop up the arena with his corpse this afternoon. Maybe you can get word to your leader to be wary of trickery—something about a wine cup, I don't know what."

"I will certainly do as you suggest," I replied. "But what is Zantor to you that you wish to save him?"

He shrugged. "He is nothing to me. But by all reports he is a gentleman and a man of honor. I despise Panchan, that gilded boy-lover, and hate to see him down the better man by vile cunning. Now throw me clear when I give the word—first, let me stoop to get my ax—*now!*"

I whirled him about and released him, making it look as if he had broken free by main force. He staggered away and vanished in the mass of struggling men, and no one, I am convinced, was the wiser. I looked about, craning my head over the embattled throng, searching for Zantor. And found him—face to face with Panchan, in the moment of challenge!

Bugles blew, ringing above the tumult, calling the throng's attention to the duel of champions. Panchan, his glorious golden body stripped naked save for scarlet loin-silk and narrow-strapped sandals, postured gracefully to the admiring crowd, held up his hand and proposed to drink a toast with Zantor to the victor in their contest. It was a noble gesture and the crowd applauded wildly. The leader of the *tharians* had brought a flask of wine and twin gold goblets, and while Zantor stood waiting with impassive mien, leaning upon his spear, the other deftly filled both goblets and proffered one of them to the leader of the spearmen with a smirk.

And suddenly I understood the import of the words Ergon had brought to me—"something about a wine cup." And terror smote me. For I knew beyond any doubt that there would be a potent drug in the wine cup from which Zantor would drink. A drug that would not take effect until the combat had been underway for some few minutes. A drug that would weaken or befuddle him, making him easy prey for the mace of Panchan, or for the slim, gold-hilted rapier that was his pride.

Desperately, I forced my way through the grunting, cursing press of embattled warriors, using elbows and knees to squeeze through to the place where Panchan and Zantor stood facing each other, cup in hand. As I fought my way through the mass of men they were just lifing their cups in a toast to each other.

There was no time for words or explanations. Lunging forward, I dashed the gold cup from Zantor's hand. And as astounded silence fell over the arena. I stood there panting, sweating under the linen headdress that covered my yellow hair from view. Zantor regarded me with a puzzled expression. But Panchan was livid with rage, his wet mouth working, eyes glaring wildly, as enraged as if it had been from his hand that I had rudely dashed the goblet.

In the next instant he raised his mace and sprang at me with a lithe, tigerish bound. Perhaps he wished to silence me as soon as possible, before I could accuse him before the arena of treacherously attempting to drug or poison his opponent.

At any rate, I found myself fighting for my life— against the most feared champion among all the gladiators of Zanadar!

Book V

AGAINST ALL ODDS

Defending myself as best I could, I backed away from Panchan's furious assault. Over his shoulder I saw Zantor looking on, his face blank with amazement at this turn of events. The battle around us stilled; the stands were a silent wall of frozen faces and staring eyes. But I was far too busy just keeping myself alive to think of anything else.

The mace of the gladiators is a heavy, cumbersome weapon which requires considerable strength of wrist to wield with any particular agility. In the hands of Panchan, though, the steel ax seemed light as a feather. It whistled shrilly, slicing the air, as he wove it in a deadly figure-eight in the air between us. It was not long before my clumsy efforts to ward off his singing blows came to grief: the glittering edge bit deep in the hard black wood, chewing off splinters. And a moment later my spear shaft broke. Panchan had chopped it in two with a deft, backhand stroke— leaving me with a shaft of broken wood a little shorter than a broom handle to defend myself against the greatest warrior who ever fought in the arena of Zanadar.

In the stands above us, the throng sucked in its breath in gloating anticipation of the kill. The mighty Panchan had only been playing with me, and now he would close in for a quick kill—by some telepathy I could read this in their staring faces and hungry eyes. And, in truth, few men had ever stood up before Panchan the Golden as long; I cannot explain why had he had not already struck me down, unless it was that the rage that blazed in him blinded him and threw him off his timing somehow. Indeed, he was shaking with fury, and his eyes were quite mad with the rage that surges up in the pampered when they are unexpectedly deprived of a favorite toy. His working, loose-lipped mouth was smeared with spittle, and he was snarling and spitting like an infuriated cat. It would almost have been funny, if it had not been a matter of life and death.

Indeed, death was very near to me now—only seconds away. Another moment and he would catch the broken stub of my spear in the hook atop the head of his mace and rip it from my grasp with a practiced twist of those iron wrists. Then it would fly up, that ax, and come whistling down to slake its scarlet thirst in my body.

There was nothing else to do—so I did the one thing Panchan could not have expected. I have often found, in moments of extreme danger, that the way out lies in doing something at total random—the last move anyone would anticipate. It has saved me from death before, this trick, and it saved me now.

Panchan advanced upon me, eyes flaming with greedy triumph, cutting the air between us with his singing blade. The only sensible and logical thing to do was to retreat cautiously, buying time, delaying the inevitable blow. *Instead, I sprang forward and thrust the sharp, splintered tip of my broken spear straight in his face.*

I had timed it beautifully, waiting until the whirling

ax had whistled past me, before darting in to thrust
the splintered stub of my spear in Panchan's startled
face.

Taken completely off guard, he winced back, turning his sullen, pretty face away from the stabbing
splinters. For a moment he lurched off guard—and in
that moment I brought the butt of my spear around
and cracked him across the forearm with a stinging
blow. He screeched, loosening numb, tingling fingers,
and the heavy mace went cartwheeling from his
nerveless grasp to thud against the arena sands a dozen
feet away.

I jabbed the broken end of my spear at him again,
and this time a splinter caught and tore his girlishly
smooth cheek, dragging a line of leaking scarlet down
it to the angle of his jaw just beneath the ear. Panchan
—bloodied!—by an ill-trained spear-slave, armed with
a *stick?* The gasp of astonishment that burst from a
thousand lips was clearly audible even above the
thunder of my heart pounding like a frightened bird
against the cage of my ribs.

His sulky face streaming with gore, distorted into a
bloody, tigerish mask of rage, he sprang lithely back-
wards and whipped his gold-hilted rapier from its
scabbard. The point sang toward me, dancing through
the air, daylight flashing from its razory edge.

But now I was in *my* element, and he had ventured
beyond the limits of his prowess. For he proved a
clumsy novice with the blade, while I may claim without false modesty to be a master-swordsman. And,
although I wielded but a broken shaft of wood, it was
about the length and very nearly of the weight of the
swords with which I had trained my skill to the heights
of artistry. He swore and sweated and stamped; I
turned aside every thrust, parried every wild swinging

blow, with effortless ease. The arena roared with wild, yelling thunder. That day of days I gave them a show such as they had never seen.

As for Panchan, he was a sorry sight, his face a mask of blood, his splendid golden body streaming sweat, smeared with dust, and dribbling gore from many small wounds, for, from time to time, my wooden shaft slid through his guard to scratch his torso lightly. And the throng loved it all! I guess part of the pleasure in applauding a champion is a furtive, secret thrill of hope that he will fail, thus redeeming the common man's instinctive fear and hatred of those superior to himself in some way or other. At any rate, Panchan's fall from the heights of popularity was fast —and far.

The thing came to an abrupt end I had not planned. In truth, I had not thought past the moment, nor envisioned any way to end the duel; I had long since lost control of events, and moved from one event to the next as seemed best.

Panchan made a frenzied lunge at me. I knocked his rapier aside and drew back my arm for a return thrust when his foot slipped in the loose sand and he flung himself forward with all his weight, impaling himself on my broken spear. A deathly silence fell like a thunderclap. I bent to touch his breast, to pick up the sword he had let fall. He would need it no more: one long splinter had gone through his heart.

I rose to my feet in the echoing silence and lifted the sword of Panchan in the victory salute. And the throng went wild.

Prince Thuton loved it little, but the chaplet of victory was mine, and although he would far rather have condemned me to a pit of deltagars, no prince reigns long who denies his people their heroes. And I was the hero of the arena that day.

Grizzled Thon the Gamesmaster gestured me forward with his baton. I strode through the cheering *keraxians* of my team to the far wall, where guards were lowering a ladder for me to ascend to the royal box. The crowd roared itself hoarse, pelting me with ribands and bunches of flowers and gems. Still trailing in one hand the sword of Panchan the Golden, I strode my way, looking neither to right nor to left, and mounted the ladder to receive the gold chaplet from Thuton's hand.

It went very much against my nature to kneel to him, but I thought it best that he should look only upon my linen headdress and averted features, rather than stand eye to eye, looking me full in the face. For Thuton of Zanadar had good reason to remember me.

I had reckoned without the protocol of princes, however. The guard captain, as I went down on one knee, frowned disapprovingly.

"Bare your head before your prince, slave!" he growled, and, swift as thought, before I could stay his hand with an involuntary gesture, bent and snatched the cloth away.

"*Jandar!*"

It was the voice of my beloved. I lifted my face and looked into her incredulous, astonished eyes. Thuton blenched and whitened.

"Jandar—?" he repeated.

My name flew from lip to lip, first in tones of wonderment, then in a ringing shout of outrage. For they knew me—my name, my strange yellow hair—I was Jandar of Callisto, that daring rogue who had bearded the Sky Pirates before in their very lair, carrying off

the princess of Shondakor from their clutches. An un-
holy glee flamed in Thuton's livid face, and his sword
rasped from its scabbard to ring against my own.

"Face to face at last, you dog!" he breathed as we
thrust and parried amid a tumultuous, shouting
crowd. "You were mad to venture on a second time
into my realm . . . this time I shall bathe my steel in
your heart's blood, and hurl your stinking carrion from
the walls of Zanadar!"

And for the second time in the same hour I found
myself fighting for my life. But this time it was sword
against sword—and Thuton was an excellent swordsman. I had few hopes of breaking through his furious,
whipping blade to strike him down with any ease, for
I was weary and he was fresh. And time was rapidly
running out; guards were sprinting for the royal box
from every post and station. At any second I could
expect a thrust from behind. But at least I would die
with a sword in my hand, facing my dearest enemy.

Darloona cried out my name in sharp warning; I
swerved, glancing over one shoulder. The guard captain—the same man who had plucked the headdress
from my brows—was about to make his thrust, and
from this proximity I knew his blade would run me
through. I also knew I could do nothing about it.

What happened next was one of those small im-
ponderable strokes of chance whose coming you can
never anticipate. I suppose it is a matter of the chem-
istry between people, or one of the mysteries of the
human heart.

For, from the arena sands below, where he stood
breathless with amazement amidst a thousand gladiators, Ergon—bald, ugly, scowling, truculent Ergon—
thundered out one word, "*Jandar!*" and flung his great
mace whirling through the air to dash out the brains

of the guard who stood behind me, about to run me
through.

And, in the next instant, Zantor, from where he
stood among my fellow *keraxians,* shouted *"Jandar!"*
and sent his great spear hissing through the air to pin
a second guard to the benches.

A thousand gladiators raised their voices in one
mighty, earth-shaking shout—"Jandar! Jandar! *Jandar!"*

And before the echoes of my name faded from the
air, the gladiators of Zanadar swarmed to the arena
wall, sprang to clutch its topmost ledge, and clambered
over into the stands. Maces swung lustily—spears
sank through chest and belly and throat—guards, who
flocked to the side of their prince, found themselves
battling a horde of warriors, with Zantor and Ergon
at their head.

The throng of spectators broke and fled in a screaming, milling, clawing tangle of struggling bodies that
impeded the guards hurrying to stem the slave rebellion and that also jammed the exits. They had come
to loll at their ease, sucking sweatmeats while men
battled and died for their momentary pleasure. They
had little stomach for playing a part in that battle
themselves.

These things I noticed in passing, catching snatches
of what was happening below in hurried glances over
my shoulder. For Thuton's flashing blade kept me busy
enough and demanded my full attention. He fought
like a maniac. His point seemed everywhere at once,
now darting for my throat, now flicking toward my
breast, now flashing to impale my wrist. And as he
fought, his slick white pasty face wet with perspiration,
his snarling mouth spewing curses of unspeakable

vileness, he drove me back inch by inch.

In the narrow confines of the royal box, amidst a tangle of draperies, treading wine goblets and smeared fruits underfoot, stumbling over cushions, I was greatly hampered and could not employ my usual style. I was forced to fight a purely defensive duel, which went against my grain, but in the whirling confusion, I watched for an opening, determining to use the secret *botte* I had learned from Lukor.

Thuton began to tire. He was an excellent swordsman with a bravura style, but years of soft foods and rich wines and luxurious living had weakened his arm and sapped his vigor. He began to puff and wheeze for breath; his face purpled with effort; his sword arm trembled with strain.

Suddenly he faltered, gasping, and his point wavered. And in that moment I had him. I lunged forward, my blade singing through the air, and its bright steel was quenched as I drove it through his putrid heart. I whipped back, and he slid off my blade and sprawled at my feet, dead as a stone.

Thus fell the last prince of the Sky Pirates of Zanadar, and thus I avenged in blood the thousand wrongs done my princess.

She stood against a fallen chair, one hand clenched at her heart, all of her soul in her glorious eyes. I strode forward and swept her into my arms, crushed her to my breast, and drank one superb kiss from her soft, warm lips. Lips that I had kissed ten thousand times in dreams and fancies . . . lips that I kissed now in living actuality for the first time!

We stood for a long moment thus, wrapped in the warm wonder of our love. The world was very far away and unimportant to us in that timeless moment of rapture. I will not set down here in cold black ink what words we whispered to each other then. Lovers have whispered such precious things since Time's dawn; I daresay we were not very original.

Then we turned, my arm about her lissom waist, to view the havoc I had wrought. The vanguard of the gladiators had cut their way to the box, and they ringed us about with a wall of steel. Guards lay sprawled in blood-splattered heaps across the benches, which were otherwise largely empty, as the bulk of the citizenry had fled. But guards were boiling out of the entranceways like ants whose nest a meddling giant has crushed. They came hurtling down the steep aisles in grim-faced ranks, to be met by a howling mob of freedom-maddened gladiators.

I turned to Darloona.

"Remain here, my princess," I commanded. "Here you will be safe."

Her voice was a husky caress. "And you, my beloved?"

"I must lend my sword to my friends," I said. "I cannot linger here while they fight and die. It was for friendship of me that they rose in rebellion, and while one of them yet lives, I shall stand by his side."

I turned from her then to join my comarades.

It was an unequal contest from the outset. Gladiators armed with wooden spears are poorly matched against guardsmen in steel helmets and breastplates, armed with the keen-bladed rapiers of Zanadar. However, we checked their rush and held them with the sheer ferocity of our assault. Men who fight for freedom fight better than men who fight for pay. However true this may be, there were many of them and few of us, and the outcome of the battle was obvious.

For a time we held them. But it could not last.

Ergon plucked at my sleeve and I turned. Battle evidently agreed with him, for his ugly face was cheerful if somewhat battered.

"Jandar—we could fall back to the floor of the arena," he suggested. "We could retire to the pits below. There they could only come at us two at a time. With a handful of gladiators, I could hold the pits till the world grows old. . . ."

Zantor strode near, his stern face merry, a smile on his grim lips.

"There is much in what you say, friend Ergon," he said. "But I have a better idea. We could strike through the north gate and reach the shipyards and steal a vessel. My own galley, the *Xaxar*, is there, impounded under the prince's seal."

"Perhaps so," Ergon grunted. "But who could fly the thing? None of us know aught of such matters, and you alone are not enough to man so huge a craft."

"No need to fret on that account," Zantor smiled. "Half my crew went into slavery with me; they served with me among the *keraxians;* they fight beside us now, in Jandar's rebellion!"

"Beware—the guards are breaking through!" a loud voice shouted over the tumult.

"Which shall it be, Jandar? Do we fall back to hold the pits—or strike for the shipyards?" demanded Ergon urgently.

But the decision was wrested from my hand by Fate!

A thunderous crash rocked the arena. Glass—glass —*glass!* It was suddenly everywhere, falling in a jagged rain. One glittering deluge swept the spearhead of the guards' assault, slashing arms, and gashing throats. Their spearhead crumpled, blunted, broke, and retired in confusion.

A black shadow swept over us. My comrades craned their necks, blinking apprehensively at the sky, and at the fantastic aerial monster that had come shattering down through the crystal dome which sheltered the arena like an enormous bowl.

Of them all, I alone knew there was naught to fear. Tension drained from me, and I laughed aloud, tossing Panchan's sword up in the air and catching it in my hand.

My friends looked upon my antics with amazement, fearing I had lost my reason. What occasion for joy and laughter could be found in the descent of one of the mighty warships of Zanadar, which even now sank towards us, blotting out the sky?

I grinned, slapping bewildered Ergon on one massive shoulder. For the road of our escape was suddenly open before us.

And the *Jalathadar* had come at last!

Chapter 14

THE DOOM OF ZANADAR

From the decks of the *Jalathadar* a withering rain of arrows swept the guardsmen in a barbed hail of death. Their lines broke into clots of fleeing men who were rapidly cut down.

Rope ladders were flung over the side, and I invited my fellow gladiators to clamber aboard. Above, I glimpsed Koja solemnly staring down at me, his great Yathoon whip-sword naked in one hand. At his shoulder, Valkar and Lukor grinned down at me. Swiftly, the gladiators swarmed up over the rail, while the Shondakorian archers stood on the foredeck, alert for a return of the guards in one last, desperate assault.

I had no notion what sequence of accidents could have delayed the arrival of the *Jalathadar* for so many days, but it could not have come at a more perfect time. Later I would be told how the treacherous Ulthar had crippled the giant ornithopter, how the gale winds had carried the helpless ship far north among the icy peaks of the Frozen Land, how the courage and gallantry of young Tomar had rooted the traitor from his hiding place, and how the crew, laboring desperately, had repaired the crippled flying gear as best they might, and limped back to Zandar. I would learn how the ship had lingered out of sight, waiting for darkness to descend, until the uproar of rebellion in the arena caught the keen eye of a lookout, who spotted my bright thatch of yellow hair and gave the signal to attack.

Zantor touched my arm.

"Let me take my men and strike out for the shipyards, Jandar," he urged. "If we take swift advantage of this unexpected diversion, we can seize the *Xaxar* and join you aloft. Two ships will prove better than one, especially if half the flying force of Zanadar follows at our heels, as I doubt not will be the case."

"Go, then," I said. "We will do what we can to cover you." He wrung my hand wordlessly and turned on his heel to marshal his men. A few moments later they were sprinting for the gate. There was no opposition. The guards had lost heart and had fled, leaving the arena in our hands.

Darloona awaited me in the royal box, where the corpse of the slain Prince Thuton lay face down in a pool of congealing gore. I caught the bottom rung of the nearest rope ladder, told her to put her arms around my neck, and climbed swiftly to the rail. As I helped her over the balustrade and stepped down to the deck beside her, a great shout of welcome rang from a hundred throats and more. I glimpsed tears in the eyes of grizzled Haakon, and Valkar's handsome face was radiant as he knelt to kiss her hand and rose to clap me on the shoulder.

The princess gazed around, smiling at familiar faces. "Is it possible that you have come all this way to save me?" she murmured faintly. Valkar smiled.

"It was Jandar's notion that we should refurbish the Sky Pirate craft captured during the attack on Shondakor and stake all on a desperate attempt to breach the defenses of Zanadar to effect your rescue, my princess," he said. "By the act of a traitor, Jandar was lost from amongst our number. I should have known that he would turn up in time for the final battle!"

I acknowledged his greetings. "Yes, but it isn't over yet! You men get to your stations, and see that these gladiators have a place amongst you. A second group is cutting a path through the streets, bound for the shipyards. We may soon be joined by yet a second ship, manned by friends."

In a trice we lifted from the corpse-strewn arena and rode the winds above the city. Zantor and his *keraxians* were halfway to the docks by now, having met with little, and disorganized, opposition en route. As they swarmed over the rail of the *Xaxar* and rapidly took up their accustomed stations, we lowered teams of axmen with instructions to do as much damage as possible to the pirate craft moored below.

It proved remarkably easy to put the enemy ships out of action. And, in this task, my fellow gladiators were very useful. For a burly *tharian*, armed with a thirty-pound mace of tempered steel, can chop a hole in a pirate hull in no time, releasing the buoyant vapors pent therein. And an ornithopter with a pierced hull and leaking gas is so much dead weight. By the time the *Xaxar* cut her cables and rose to join us aloft, not a ship in port was sky-worthy.

But not all of the Zanadarian fleet had lain in moorage; a half-dozen or more scout frigates circled the mountaintop city at various levels of altitude, and it did not take them long to learn the city was under attack. One swept toward us, lean prow cutting the windy sky.

"Now we shall see just how well my 'secret weapon' works in battle," I remarked to Valkar. "Or have you already found occasion to give my catapult its baptism of fire?"

"Not yet," he laughed. "But we shall see how well it works soon enough! Catapult crew—to your stations!"

The covering was shorn away and the giant bow unlimbered. Crewmen fitted one of the great, six-pound steel arrows into place and made ready to launch it at the enemy craft now swooping toward us. The effective range of the weapon was three hundred yards, but that is the outside limit, and, having flown that far, the barbed steel-bolts have expended most of their momentum and might not have enough force left to punch through the laminated paper hull. Thus Valkar waited until the enemy ship was within two hundred yards—which was dangerously close—before giving the command to release the catapult. The first enemy arrows were plunking into the decks about us as the mighty catapult discharged its first missile.

The steel arrow was a blur as it hissed through empty air to crunch into the hull of the corsair craft. My warriors raised a lusty shout of triumph as the arrow punched a gaping hole in the hull. A ragged cry went up from the decks of the foe, but it was drowned in the scream of escaping gases. Suddenly no longer buoyant, the corsair ship wobbled drunkenly and sank, passing beneath us.

But we had no time to trace its fall with gloating eyes, for the second pirate was almost upon us, followed closely by two more. Frantically, Valkar's crew cranked the catapult up again until the taut bow sang with tension. One crewman gasped, and slapped at his upper arm, suddenly transfixed by an arrow from the approaching craft. He staggered back, his place eagerly taken by a broad-chested ex-gladiator. With a deep moaning whine we fired a second bolt from the giant bow.

Like a steel thunderbolt it slammed into the bow of the oncoming corsair and snapped the keel in two parts—an amazingly lucky shot, with the most unexpected results! This keel, you see, holds the fabric together. Once broken, the ship began to break apart under its own internal stresses. For while the ship has no real weight, because of the buoyant gas held under pressure in the double hull, it has mass and it is cumbersome due to its size.

The second ship literally broke in half in midair. Howling men fell over the rail, dwindling black motes that receded into the misty gulfs below. The ship sagged drunkenly and fell, crumbling apart into a rain of gigantic fragments. Again, my warriors raised a hearty cheer.

By this time the *Xaxar* was aloft, and Zantor had already engaged the third enemy ship, while we cranked up the catapult and fired another bolt at the fourth. But the Sky Pirates were becoming wary of my new weapon and veered aside just in time. The steel bolt hissed past their prow, narrowly missing it. This fourth ship, and a fifth one whose approach I had not noticed, began circling us, careful to avoid the catapult.

Zantor, of course, had only conventional weapons, but his knowledge of this new art of aerial warfare was superior to mine, and he dispatched his adversary

in a novel and most decisive manner. I had wondered
whether or not the gas trapped in the double hull of
the flying galleons might not be flammable and even
explosive, assuming it to be a gas like hydrogen. Zantor confirmed my guess by arming his men with fire
arrows. Six or seven of their burning shafts sank harm-
lessly in the hull of the third Zanadarian craft before
a lucky eighth shot penetrated the double hull and
ignited the vapors in it.

The entire prow of the enemy ship vanished in a
deafening thunderclap and a ball of blazing flame.
The rest of the ship, a seething inferno, plunged to its
doom.

Now we engaged our two wary adversaries with
hastily devised fire arrows, which were ordinary shafts,
whose barbed tips were bound with a bit of greasy
waste, set afire by coals fetched from the galley. In no
time a fifth ship went screaming down in flames. As
for the sixth, it blundered within range of the catapult,
and sank to crash on the fanglike peaks of the mountains far below, a gaping hole in its hull.

And thus the first aerial battle in the history of
Thanator was concluded. In twenty minutes, or a bit
less, we had downed six ships and cleared the skies
of foemen.

In the engagement precisely one Shondakorian had
been injured when an arrow pierced his upper arm.
The shaft had been removed, the wound sponged
clean and smeared with salve and bandaged, and the
man was in good humor, joking with his comrades.

We circled the mountaintop city in preparation for
our departure. And it was one of my former fellow
gladiators who gave me the key to rendering the Sky
Pirates helpless to avenge our attack. This fellow had
been a slave in the gas mines before being condemned

to the arena for striking a guard who had sought to whip one of his friends to death for some minor infraction of the rules.

He pointed out the gas mines to me; they were on the crest of the mountain, just below the peak where the arena and the palace citadel of the Zanadarian rulers were situated. It seems that the mountain held vast pockets of buoyant gas, which the Zanadarians had capped with massive iron valves. My informant did not need to point out what an excellent diversionary tactic to cover our escape it would be if we could knock off one of these valves and ignite the escaping gas.

The feat could best be left to a *tharian*. I explained the scheme to the assembled crew and called for volunteers from among the former gladiators. I was a bit disconcerted to see that it was my friend Ergon who was the first to step forward.

His great mace slung over his shoulder in a hastily jury-rigged baldric, we lowered him on a line to the row of stone chimneys, after first sweeping the scene with arrows, driving away the mine guards. With our hearts in our mouths we watched from the hovering ship as Ergon's tiny figure clung to the top of one chimney, beating the massive valve askew with ringing blows of his great mace.

It seemed to take forever. Darkness had already fallen, the swift quenching of the sourceless golden radiance that is the Thanatorian equivalent of daylight. The world was thrust suddenly into darkness, save for the dim, enormous globe that was the orange-banded giant planet Jupiter, thrusting his luminous orb over the horizon. In the sudden dark, enemy craft could descend upon us unseen. Our danger increased with every moment we remained here.

And then Ergon came swinging back up the line,

purple-faced and blowing from his exertions. Wiping his brow and downing a hearty swig of strong brandy, he cheerfully informed us we could loose our fire arrows at will.

At my command a rank of Shondakorian archers took up their stations. Grease-impregnated rags knotted about their shafts just behind the arrowheads themselves were touched to flame by coals fetched from the galley. The burning arrows traced arcs of orange flame against the night.

"It's no good," Haakon growled. "The winds are too strong, they extinguish every arrow."

"Be patient," I counseled him.

The dozenth arrow did the trick. Suddenly night was turned to day as an incredible fountain of white-hot flame gushed from the shattered valve. The jet of flame spouted five hundred feet into the air and blazed above the city like a glowing plume.

Valkar seized my arm.

"Look!" he shouted, pointing. I followed his gaze and saw black cracks zigzag between the valve-capped chimneys. Then a subterranean rumbling filled the air, as if some great beast was pent within the mountain, growling for its freedom. Dazzlement smote our eyes as the valve which capped the second chimney exploded releasing a jet of scorching fury. And a third —and a fourth!

I ordered the *Jalathadar* to ascend a thousand feet above the mountaintop city. The *Xaxar*, circling near, followed our example. And just in time! For in the next instant a deafening explosion shook the city of the Sky Pirates, and, in the fierce light which beat from the immense fireball which blazed up from the gas mines, we saw that the entire summit of the peak was splitting apart, huge fragments spinning slowly away. By the glare we saw even more astounding

sights: the lofty towers of Zanadar were toppling
slowly, all in a row, like stacks of toy building-blocks
shoved by an enormous, unseen hand.

Another terrific explosion shook the mountain of the
Sky Pirates, hiding the city on the summit from our
view behind a roiling cloud of inky black smoke, shot
through with flames of sulphurous crimson. The flying ship rocked suddenly as a vast chunk of rock went
spinning past us.

The frigid gale winds whipped the black smoke
away in long, ragged streamers that trailed across the
sky. With astonishment, and more than a touch of cold
horror, we saw that the explosion had undermined
the city, which was constructed in ascending levels,
topped with the palace citadel and the great arena itself. Now that the smoke of the explosion was whipped
away we could see that the arena was gone entirely,
and the central guard-barracks as well, and, even as
we stared, the mighty palace citadel was crumbling.
Walls peeled away, coming apart in slow motion,
rushing into the fiery crater that had been the gas
mines in heavy landslides of crushed rock. Half the
palace dissolved in roaring avalanches of broken stone
even as we watched.

The mountain shuddered to the thunder of explo-
sions that resounded deep within its heart. Flaming
incandescent gas boiled in a vast plume from the
black-edged crater. Walls buckled, buildings collapsed,
towers fell, blocking the streets with rubble.

We stood silently on the windswept deck and without words we watched the death of a city. It had been
a city of our enemies, but few among us were so callous as to gloat in triumph over the hideous doom
that enveloped Zanadar. Thousands lay dead in the
smoking wreckage; hundreds more were injured. In a
thousand years, the Zanadarians could never rebuild

their civilization to the heights of power they had so cruelly enjoyed. Never again would the aerial corsairs of the City in the Clouds bring terror and despair to the lesser cities of Thanator. Their reign was ended, and it closed in a roaring holocaust of belching flame, shattering stone, and earthquake.

We could look no longer on such scenes of devastation. The *Jalathadar* swung about into the wind and circled once above the smoldering funeral pyre that had been a city. With the *Xaxar* trailing behind us, we turned away from the scene of doom and ruin.

"Is it south, Jandar?" Koja inquired solemnly. I nodded.

"It is south, down across the jungle countries to Golden Shondakor," I said.

My arm was about the slim shoulders of my princess. I bent to kiss her lips, and again the warriors raised my name in a mighty shout of triumph and victory.

I was very tired.

And I was going home.

Chapter 15

THE THRONE OF SHONDAKOR

Whenever night falls across the Jungle Moon, and the titan orb of Jupiter the giant planet swims into the skies with all its train of attendant moons, I marvel again at the inexplicable whim of destiny that has brought me to this alien world for some unknown and inscrutable purpose I cannot even guess.

What other man of my race has experienced adventures so harrowing, viewed marvels of such magnitude, wandered upon so fantastic a world of wonder and terror and beauty?

I sit in the palace of Shondakor, writing these words on crackling parchment with a pen cut from a thaptor quill. Soon this third volume of my memoirs on the mystery world of Thanator will be finished. Ere long, a Ku Thad war party will venture forth from the city, cross the Grand Kumala, and lay this manuscript on the immense disk of milky jade that is the Gate Between the Worlds. Sometime thereafter a strange beam of sparkling force will arch against the sky, traveling through the black infinitude of space, transporting this book to the ruined stone city in the jungles of Cambodia on distant Earth.

The Earth I shall doubtless never see again. For, although I dearly love that far-off planet upon which I was born, the fates have carried me from thence to mysterious Callisto, three hundred and eighty-seven million, nine hundred and thirty thousand miles from the world of my birth.

And here, on this strange and alien world of golden skies and scarlet jungles, of weird races and ferocious monsters, here I have truly come home.

For here on Callisto I have at last found a cause to fight for and gallant comrades to fight at my side and foemen worthy of my steel. Here on Callisto I have found the woman that I love. The woman that is now my wife, and who will ere long be the mother of my strong sons and lovely daughters.

I do not regret the world I leave behind; and yet I find it curiously difficult to sever myself from her and her ways. I have had the unique fortune to traverse the gulf between the planets and to be the first of my race to discover that life truly does exist upon the surface of alien worlds. This message is of such transcendent importance that I feel I owe it to mankind to inform it of my discovery. And for that reason I have laboriously set down an account of my wanderings and exploits on the Jungle Moon, although I shall never know for certain if my words have reached the men of my birth-world, or if they wander lost somewhere in the black gulfs that gape and yawn between the cold and silent stars.

Down across the immense region of the Grand Kumala we flew, our twin ships traversing the skies of Thanator with ease. At length, after a voyage of some days, the walls and towers of Golden Shondakor emerged from the mists of the horizon and we circled downward through the brilliant morn.

In their thousands the Ku Thad people were there to greet us and to welcome us home after our hazardous adventure half a world away. They lined the rooftops and the balconies; they stood beside the broad stone-paved boulevards, lifting their faces toward us. And when at length we emerged from our vessels, and the people of Shondakor beheld the red-gold mane of their lost princess, ten thousand flags and banners burst from tower top and roof and spire and a mighty roar of welcome came thundering from a hundred thousand hearts.

Lord Yarrak was there to press his beloved niece and queen to his breast. She mounted with him into a golden chariot drawn by a team of thaptors, and then turned and held out her hand to me, and I mounted and stood beside her. We rode slowly through streets lined with cheering thousands. It was a greeting reserved for conquering heroes. I felt very much at home.

To the gates of the palace we rode, and, within the great hall, we watched with joy and pride in our hearts as Princess Darloona mounted the great flight to stone steps to the throne dais. There, not long ago, the black idol, Hoom, god of the Chac Yuul, had crouched in all his hideousness. Now the great gold throne of Shondakor had been restored to its place once more, and we watched as the warrior princess of the Ku Thad took her place upon that throne. As one, we whipped our swords from their scabbards and a hundred blades flashed aloft in the royal salute.

And there, on that same dais, some ten days later, before a glittering throng of the assembled nobles and warriors of the realm, Darloona became my bride. The ceremony was a simple one. No priest officiated, for the people of Thanator in general do not seem to venerate any gods save the shadowy and mysterious Lords of Gordrimator, who dwell, it is said, upon the glowing surface of mighty Jupiter.

Tears of happiness stung my eyes as I folded my wife in my arms, then turned to receive the salute and the plaudits of our kingdom. The domed roof rang with our shouted names as we stood smiling down upon the faces of all our old and gallant and trusted friends—kingly Lord Yarrak and the wise old sage Zastro, huge solemn-eyed Koja and white-bearded Lukor, valiant young Tomar and noble Valkar, ugly Ergon and tall Zantor.

Thus were we wed; thus I became Prince of Shondakor!

It seems unlikely that any foe will again disturb the peace of the Golden City. The Black Legion is broken, decimated, and dispersed; the Sky Pirates have been robbed of their fleet; and their city lies in smoking rubble. There is no reason why the Yathoon Horde or the Bright Empire of Perushtar should turn against us in war. The last of our enemies has been defeated. We are now the single most powerful kingdom upon the known surface of Thanator, what with our own small aerial navy, the *Jalathadar* and the *Xaxar*, who float aloft, tethered to the spires of the palace.

But who knows what the future may bring? The other hemisphere of the Jungle Moon is a shadowy realm of mystery, whereof we know little. And unknown foemen may dwell about the far shores of the Lesser Sea or amidst the cold wastes of the Frozen Land.

We must wait to see what tomorrow will bring. But as for myself, I have no fear. I have won the heart of the loveliest woman in two worlds; I have gained the throne of the most powerful kingdom upon this planet; all her enemies I have defeated, broken, and scattered. Let tomorrow bring what tomorrow will bring—I will face it unafraid.

If there be any on the world of my birth who read these words, to you I send my greetings. Amidst the starry immensities of the universe, you are not alone. On the strange surface of a distant world, a man of your race stands, extending to you the hand of friendship and brotherhood across the depths of space.

The day may yet come, my unknown friend, when we shall stand together, you and I, in battle against unknown foes.

To you, my salute, and greeting, and—farewell!

—*Jandar of Callisto*
Prince of Shondakor

Appendix

GLOSSARY OF CHARACTERS IN THE CALLISTO BOOKS

ARKOLA: warlord of the Chac Yuul or Black Legion.

ASHULOK: one of the merchant princes of Narouk.

BLUTO: a guardsman of the Chac Yuul in Shondakor.

CHAM: a lord of the House of Iskelion in Narouk.

DARJAN: pseudonym adopted by Jandar while a slave in Narouk and a gladiator in Zanadar.

DARLOONA: warrior princess of the Ku Thad, beloved of Jandar.

ERGON: a Perushtarian slave who fought among the gladiators of Zanadar and became Jandar's friend.

EYKOR: young aristocrat of Zanadar; one of the students of Lukor's academy.

FARZEMUM: a merchant prince of Narouk.

GAMCHAN: Koja's rival among the chieftains of the Yathoon Horde.

GAMEL: servitor of Lord Cham of Narouk.

GAMELION: a former ruler of Shondakor; in the second of the Callisto Books, Jandar attends a performance in a theater bearing his name.

GOLAR: valet to Prince Vaspian of the Chac Yuul.

GRYPHAR: father of Prince Thuton and founder of the dynasty of Zanadar.

HAAKON: a Shondakorian officer aboard the *Jalathadar*.

HOOM: hideous stone idol worshiped by the Chac Yuul.

IDOLON: one of the merchant princes of Glorious Perusht in whose household Ergon was raised.

IMARRA: a slave in the household of Lord Cham.

IRIVOR: one of Lukor's friends in the days when he taught swordsmanship in Zanadar.

JANDAR: Captain Jonathan Andrew Dark, an American soldier of fortune.

KAAMURATH: Seraan of Soraba.

KAMAD: inventor of the secret *botte* Lukor taught to Jandar, knowledge of which makes one an invincible swordsman.

KAMCHAN: supreme overlord of the Yathoon Horde.

KANELON: a slave in the household of Lord Cham.

KOJA: a chieftain of the Yathoon Horde who became Jandar's first friend on Callisto.

LOGUAR: an officer of the Chac Yuul.

LUKOR: a master-swordsman from Ganatol who befriended Jandar during his first adventure in Zanadar.

LYKON: pseudonym adopted by Jandar while he lived in the house of Lukor in Zanadar.

MARADOL: a former ruler of Zanadar.

MARAK: young aristocrat of Zanadar, one of Lukor's pupils.

MARUD: an innkeeper of Shondakor who served as a Ku Thad spy during the occupation of that city by the Black Legion.

MURRAK: a senior commander of the Legion.

NARGA: a guard captain of the Legion, on palace duty during the last days of Arkola's regime.

OOL THE UNCANNY: one of the dreaded Mind Wizards of Kuur, who had gained a powerful voice in the councils of the Chac Yuul during the last days of their occupation of Shondakor.

PANDOL: high chief of the clan in which Koja was a chieftain.

PANCHAN THE GOLDEN: popular favorite among the gladiators of Zanadar.

SORASTO: a playwright of earlier times; the Shakespear of Thanator. Jandar attended a performance of one of his plays in the second of the Callisto Books.

SUJAT: a member of Koja's retinue when Jandar was enslaved among the Yathoon Horde. It was Sujat who taught Jandar the common language spoken on Thanator.

THON: Gamesmaster of the arena of Zanadar.

THUTON: ruler of Zanadar.

TOMAR: a youth who served aboard the *Jalathadar*.

ULTHAR: former corsair captain taken prisoner by the Shondakorians.

URUSH: a noble of Soraba.

VALKAR: Lord Yarrak's son; a Prince of Shondakor formerly betrothed to Darloona.

VASPIAN: son of the warlord Arkola and prince of the Chac Yuul among whose retinue Jandar briefly served as described in the second of the Callisto Books.

WARLAK THE MAD: a former ruler of Zanadar who, in his madness, constructed the maze of secret passages within the walls of the palace citadel.

YANTHAR: a guardsman of Zanadar.

YARRAK: Darloona's uncle; the senior peer of Shondakor.

ZANTOR: a former corsair captain who became Jandar's friend when both served among the gladiators of Zanadar.

ZASTRO: wise Shondakorian philosopher who serves as one of Darloona's advisors.

PROTECTOR
LARRY NIVEN

Phssthpok the Pak had been travelling for most of his 32,000 years – his mission, to save, develop and protect the group of Pak breeders sent out into space some 2½ million years before . . .

Brennan was a Belter, the product of a fiercely independent, somewhat anarchic society living in, on, and around an outer asteroid belt. The Belters were rebels one and all, and Brennan was a smuggler. The Belt worlds had been tracking the Pak ship for days – Brennan figured to meet that ship first . . .

He was never seen again – at least not in the form of homo sapiens.

Larry Niven is the author of **Ringworld** which won both the Hugo and Nebula awards for the best s.f. novel of the year.

The Radiant Dome

CHALLENGE FROM THE STARS ...

Perry Rhodan had returned from the moon in Spaceship Stardust accompanied by two of the Arkonides. But the earth was on the verge of an atomic conflict. So Perry Rhodan, Peacelord of the Universe, threw an impregnable forcefield around the Stardust and declared his ship independent of the warring nations.

As he had hoped, the holocaust was temporarily averted by the more deadly threat of his allies from the stars; but could Perry Rhodan keep the peace long enough to persuade the Arkonides that mankind was fit to enter their galactic community?

THE RADIANT DOME is the second novel in the world's bestselling S.F. series. Don't miss Perry Rhodan's first cosmic adventure, ENTERPRISE STARDUST.